"What'll you give me if I say yes?" Kipp asked in his sexiest voice.

"Well, a doctor's time *is* valuable," Stacy said. "What did you have in mind?"

"For openers, I want to chase you around your classroom with the kids shouting 'dirty old man' or 'masher' at me. Then I want to catch you, grab your cute little derriere, and smooch. I've always had this thing about chasing a pretty teacher around the room."

"You're incorrigible." But she felt her heart beat faster at the thought of fulfilling his fantasy. "How about a home-cooked meal Friday night?" she offered in a soft drawl.

"Is that the best offer? Well, okay, but don't do anything about dessert. I have a few ideas of my own about that," he said, his voice full of sensual promise.

She couldn't wait. . . .

WHAT ARE *LOVESWEPT* ROMANCES?

They are stories of true romance and touching emotion. We believe those two very important ingredients are constants in our highly sensual and very believable stories in the *LOVESWEPT* line. Our goal is to give you, the reader, stories of consistently high quality that may sometimes make you laugh, sometimes make you cry, but are always fresh and creative and contain many delightful surprises within their pages.

Most romance fans read an enormous number of books. Those they truly love, they keep. Others may be traded with friends and soon forgotten. We hope that each *LOVESWEPT* romance will be a treasure—a "keeper." We will always try to publish

LOVE STORIES YOU'LL NEVER FORGET
BY AUTHORS YOU'LL ALWAYS REMEMBER

The Editors

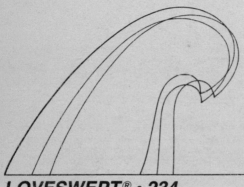

LOVESWEPT® • 234

Doris Parmett
Stiff Competition

BANTAM BOOKS
TORONTO • NEW YORK • LONDON • SYDNEY • AUCKLAND

STIFF COMPETITION

A Bantam Book / February 1988

*LOVESWEPT® and the wave device are registered
trademarks of Bantam Books. Registered in U.S. Patent
and Trademark Office and elsewhere.*

*If you would be interested in receiving protective vinyl
covers for your Loveswept books, please write to this address
for information:*

*Loveswept
Bantam Books
P.O. Box 985
Hicksville, NY 11802*

ISBN 0-553-21877-8

Published simultaneously in the United States and Canada

---

*Bantam Books are published by Bantam Books, a division
of Bantam Doubleday Dell Publishing Group, Inc. Its trademark, consisting of the words "Bantam Books" and the
portrayal of a rooster, is Registered in U.S. Patent and
Trademark Office and in other countries. Marca Registrada.
Bantam Books, 666 Fifth Avenue, New York, New York 10103.*

PRINTED IN THE UNITED STATES OF AMERICA

O   0 9 8 7 6 5 4 3 2 1

To the three Rs in my life:
  My husband, Richard
  My son, Randy
  And in loving memory of my daughter, Robin

One

Stacy Conklin dug her bare toe into the deep plush pile carpet. She had run in from the yard to answer the phone and was making no effort to conceal her rising agitation with her caller.

"Bev," she said, her voice low and ominous with warning, "if you dare mention the word *hunk* to me once more, I'm going to hang this phone up in your ear! I was married to one, remember? Look where that got me! Enough is enough. I know you mean well, but men are definitely not on my agenda."

"Oh, Stacy, don't be like that," Bev said. "The rumors from my spies are that he's *very* nice. I'll find out which house he bought in case you change your mind." Her tone was light now.

"Don't do me any favors."

"All right, but I think you're running in the wrong direction. This is modern America, for goodness' sake. Marriages break up all the time. Take your wedding ring off and let people know you're divorced and available."

"I am not available," Stacy snapped. "I've got my

1

teaching, my writing, and this house to take care of. That's more than enough, and besides, it's safe!"

They'd been all through this argument countless times. Much as she loved Bev, Stacy's feelings of guilt and frustration over her own failed marriage permeated her soul like a chronic illness. Right now she was in remission. She didn't need another flare-up!

She heard the high-pitched squeals of Bev's two-year-old Jeff in the background that Bev said she couldn't ignore. It was hard not to spoil the irrepressible tyke. Stacy sighed. The closest she would ever come to motherhood now would be as teacher to her twenty-two eager third graders.

Waiting for Bev to calm her active son, Stacy idly glanced around the knotty-pine den. With the back of her sweaty palm she absentmindedly brushed away the stray wisps of honey-blonde hair at the corner of her mouth. Once it would have irked the twenty-seven-year-old to see the home of her dreams look like anything less than a layout in *House Beautiful*. Now she no longer cared that she might be tracking in dirt, or sporting nails begging to be hidden under Lee's imitations, or that her hair wasn't meticulously groomed.

Not now. Not anymore. Not since her husband walked out on her. Well, jogged out, to be precise!

Harry, her blond Adonis, the life of the party, was intensely proud of his lean figure. He had kept trim and fit through daily morning jogging—jogging that took him right into the boudoir of the oh-so-rich gay divorcée Mona Beckman, who jogged on a king-size bed right along with him! And when Mona moved, she took dear old till-death-do-us-part forever-yours Harry with her.

Forever had lasted four years!

"Furthermore," Stacy said, picking up her line of reasoning the moment Bev returned to the phone, "I'm not interested in being available. With or without a husband, a wedding ring affords me a certain amount of protection from males with a one-track mind. When and if I ever change my mind, I'll let you know. In the meantime you and Vito are still sworn to secrecy."

"Oh, for goodness' sake," Bev countered in peppery tones, "stop judging every man by your ex. You always were blind where he was concerned. Didn't it ever seem strange to you he changed jobs three times in four years and was always trying to be the life of the party?"

"Of course. Don't you think it irks me to realize what a blind, naïve fool I was? If Harry hadn't jogged home and announced we were married too young and he wanted 'space,' "—she despised that word—"I'd probably still be washing out his damn jockstraps!"

The persistent clanging of the brass eagle door-knocker interrupted their discussion. "Sorry, toots, I've got to run. Someone's banging on the door. Kiss Vito and the holy terror for me."

She hung up and hurriedly retied the tails of her faded blue shirt into a tighter knot against her bare midriff. She was dressed for gardening, not company, and the skimpy, equally faded, blue denim cutoff shorts she wore barely cupped her buttocks.

Annoyed at the insistent knocking, she yelled to the person attached to the hand on the other side of the door, "Hold your horses, whoever you are. I'm not deaf."

She could have sworn she heard a chuckle as she hastily opened the oak door. The unwelcome stranger nonchalantly leaning against the doorjamb eclipsed the sun's glare. She was five feet five and he made her feel tiny. He was a great big shaggy bear of a man, at least six foot three, and with broad shoulders so that she could imagine the exuberant boys in her class screeching, "Wow! Paul Bunyan!"

Amber glints shot through the thick brown hair flopping over an Adidas headband. A faint stubble of beard covered his suntanned face and shadowed the long creases on either side of his mouth. It was the cleft in his chin that delighted her, though, for it made him look like a complete rogue. She guessed his age to be in the mid-thirties. There was no way to deny this was one powerfully handsome man.

Her gaze slithered down his long legs, then climbed back up again of its own volition, passing over a trim waistline and a broad expanse of chest, traveling by dark chest hairs curling over the tattered neckline of an off-white T-shirt and coming to rest on two electric blue eyes engaged in a pleasurable game of tit-for-tat.

While she completed her inspection, his shamefully twinkling eyes were steaming over her with disrobing intensity. A dark eyebrow arched appreciatively as its owner blatantly continued to measure Stacy's size-eight proportions in her skimpy outfit.

Then he grinned and the sun blazed again, gleaming on pearly white teeth between very masculine lips.

Forget Paul Bunyan! a voice warned Stacy. This was the wolf sniffing in the doorway of Grandma's house and she was Little Red Riding Hood.

One very large hand held an empty plastic measuring cup thrust in her direction.

"Hi, is your mother home?" the man asked, his voice deep, his tone good-naturedly teasing.

Stacy's snapped to attention. Her brows knitted in

displeasure. She didn't think his trite old-as-the-hills come-on was in good taste.

A memory of something familiar, something unpleasant, struggled for recognition. Slowly, as if swimming through the murky waters of her subconscious, a dawning awareness grew and then hit her in her solar plexus. Her jaw dropped. Her heart pumped at double force. She was sweating, and it wasn't from the sun.

The stranger with the electric blue eyes, the twinkling smile, and the devilish quirk of his lips was wearing the exact same kind and color warm-up suit that Harry had worn the day he'd jogged out of her life!

Awash with the sudden reliving of the nightmarish end to her marriage, Stacy reacted angrily to his question.

"My mother is not at home!"

She slammed the oak door, but not before she saw a look of astonishment wipe the smile from the handsome man's face. In the old days she'd have been aghast at her rudeness, if she'd shown any rudeness at all. But this was no longer the old days. No sir. Now she was going to do exactly as she pleased whenever she pleased!

She tramped back through the house and out into the backyard. Eyes stinging, she grabbed the trowel from the basket where she had stashed it before she went into the house and attacked her flower bed with renewed vengeance.

With every whack at the hard sun-caked August earth, she took out her anger both for the man's childish line and for not having the money to hire a professional gardener. She looked at her hands and saw the pitiful condition of her nails. What was happening to her?

She gouged out the dry ground and sent hard chips of dirt flying into the air, narrowly missing her eyes. Never again would she trust a man.

Not with her body!

Not with her mind!

Not with her salary!

"Say, aren't you afraid that you'll slice the roots, hacking into those flowers that way?"

Stacy's head reared up. A dirt-smudged hand tattooed a trail on her forehead as she squinted into the bright sun. Him again! His big frame moved to shadow her face, and she fired off her question.

"How'd you get in here?"

Gesturing toward the stockade fence, he answered simply, "The gate was open."

Cute. Code of the Old West. Open ranges! "Well, on your way out you can just close it." *And take that lousy sweat suit out of my sight forever,* she added silently.

"I'll be glad to."

Stacy watched and waited, but the jogger didn't move. He seemed to be making his mind up about something. Plunking the empty plastic measuring cup on the redwood picnic table, he pulled out one of the benches, sat down, and stretched his legs. He looked, she thought murderously, as if he were waiting for her to offer him a cold drink.

"Tell me, are you hard of hearing?" She was being nasty, but she didn't care.

"Not in the least," he replied pleasantly, and continued smiling at her. "I just thought maybe you reconsidered your earlier behavior." The words rolled off his tongue with the patience of a parent reasoning with a recalcitrant child.

"My earlier behavior!" She was amazed at his audacity. The nerve of the man! If there had been the remotest possibility that she would have felt sorry for her actions, the calm way this oaf practically demanded an apology from her in her own backyard would have killed it!

Stacy scrambled up quickly. So did her shorts. His eyes left her face and she was suddenly conscious of her scanty attire. Embarrassed, she made a valiant effort to lengthen the hem of her cutoffs, but she only succeeded in creating a sloppy fringe of the end threads. She felt her face redden at the man's amused look. He appeared to be dug in for the duration—and obviously enjoying her discomfort!

Giving up the futile attempt at modesty, she tilted her chin and dug her hands into her waistband. But standing so close to him was her second mistake. He took full advantage of his bird's-eye view of her damp shirt and her clearly outlined breasts.

The big oaf specialized in broad-daylight voyeurism! Irritated, she considered calling the police, then discarded the idea. She'd appear ridiculous. He hadn't lain a hand on her. He hadn't even raised his voice. She had! What would she charge him with? Illegal sitting on her redwood bench? Illegal assault with a measuring cup? So much for calling the boys in blue!

Stacy glowered at him, wishing his magnetic blue eyes would take an interest in the roses that were having heat stroke instead of her chest. "Why did you knock on my door?" she asked.

"Actually, it wasn't my idea."

She glanced around. "Then—?"

"Millie wants to bake me a cake." His thumb indicated the house beyond the fence. "I want to jog before it gets too hot." He grinned boyishly. "Borrowing seemed a simple way of saving time by not driving over to the supermarket. And since I'm your new neighbor . . ." His words trailed off and his eyes twinkled mischievously.

"Neighbor?"

Bev's phone call! Could it be she stumbled on Bev's mystery man? She almost laughed aloud. Oh, Bev. Poor misinformed Bev. For once her friend's spies had goofed. The new find was very much married! His wife even baked him cakes in this fierce heat.

The stranger shifted his position and looked at her for a long moment. He seemed genuinely surprised. "I've rented the place next-door for this whole year. Didn't you know?"

"No."

"If it eases your mind any, I only borrow sugar from my next-door neighbor."

It most certainly didn't ease her mind. This man spelled trouble with a capital *T*. It only proved how bad her present state of mind was. To have neighbors move out and new ones move in without her knowing was surprising. Surely she was quickly becoming a candidate for the loony bin!

"I'm Kipp Palmer." He grinned again and she watched his cleft deepen. "You see, my intentions are quite honorable."

Not quite, Stacy thought. *Millie, I've got a flash for you. Your dear husband's eyes aren't faithful and I'll just bet the rest of him isn't either*!

"And you're?" Kipp prompted her.

Stacy stared at the hand extended in introduction. It was strong and large, with long, tapered fingers and cleaner fingernails than hers. *Pick it up, or you'll make an idiot of yourself again*, she thought.

"Stacy Conklin."

"There, that wasn't so hard." She felt his hand around hers. She tried to extricate her hand only to find Kipp increasing the pressure as if to make sure she didn't go anywhere.

His next sentence threw her for a loop and sent her heartbeat into overdrive. "I'm looking forward to meeting your husband soon."

"You can't," she blurted out, and immediately could have cut out her tongue.

"I can't?"

"No." She shook her head for emphasis. Not daring to meet his questioning look, she focused her eyes on the alligator logo of Kipp's shirt. "He travels constantly. We see each other mainly on the weekends."

"Where does he travel?"

"Europe. The Middle East. Wherever." She waved her hand in an expansive gesture to include the entire world. Suddenly the thought of sending Harry off into the stratosphere was delicious. She should have included space as well, she mused. Pursing her lips to refrain from giggling, she caught the predatory glint in Kipp's eyes. Her eyesight was keen, and she did not miss his message.

"And he comes home on weekends?" Kipp asked. "Isn't it hard on him?"

"He flies the Concorde," she improvised with a flash of pure inspiration.

"He must have one heck of a strong constitution. The Concorde doesn't land in Newark. The drive from Kennedy Airport to Jersey is no picnic in itself. That alone can take two hours in traffic. . . ." His voice trailed off on a note of genuine admiration.

"I know." She deepened her tone, hoping to add just the right tinge of wifely concern. "Very often I meet him and we stay at a motel on Long Island for the weekend. When he does come home, I insist that he rest." It sounded so romantic, she was ready to puke.

"You mean you don't let him out?"

Was he laughing at her? From his deadpan expression it was impossible to tell. He covered his mouth and coughed politely. She wondered if her nose was growing longer from her lies. She felt cornered. Rivulets of perspiration etched salty paths in the valley between her breasts.

"You know how it is," she began again, intending to embellish her story with convincing detail. "We've been married only a few years. He doesn't like to be away too long. I'm sure you feel the same way about Millie." Lowering her eyelashes demurely, she smiled, sure that she sounded like a besotted bride. *There*, she thought smugly, *let him think she and her husband couldn't keep their hands off each other.* Kipp Palmer was one wolf she'd keep from her door. She'd well and truly tossed the ball into his court.

"Well, I believe in the good neighbor policy." He lobbed his return so smoothly, she didn't realize it was a trick shot. "So I'll just check up on you from time to time and see if maybe there's something I can do for you, while—?"

"Harry."

"While Harry is out of town."

Eyes wide, she cemented a smile into position. She willed herself to breathe calmly. *Get rid of him*, a stern voice warned, *or you'll give truth to the notion that blondes are dumb!*

"I wouldn't dream of bothering you," she said briskly. She jerked her hand out of his, brushing her palms on the sides of her shorts. "Here, let me have this." Reaching over, she hooked her dirty pinkie into the handle of the measuring cup, not noticing that her hand trembled slightly. "Wait here, I'll be right back."

She may as well face it, she scolded herself, the quicker she got rid of him, the less time he'd have to snoop. She wasn't going to waste time with social niceties and ask him where he and his wife lived before. She didn't give a damn.

As she fled into her French country kitchen, where once Harry did almost all the cooking—she had even lost her resident chef!—she heard the heavy tread of the stranger's footsteps behind her. He must be deaf, she decided. Either that or he was so self-centered he didn't care when someone asked him to wait.

She dashed to the sink and hastily washed her hands, not stopping to dry them. She decided not to take her stepstool out of the broom closet to help her reach the impractically high cabinet above the L-shaped island work counter. She thought she could just get the damn sugar and get rid of him!

Stretching up on her tiptoes she felt around for the seldom used sugar canister. As she groped blindly, her slippery fingers barely made contact with it.

"Don't you want help with that?" Kipp casually leaned a hip against the door. Stubbornly shaking her head no, she didn't see the wide smile on his face as he watched her lithe form strain against her clothes.

Her neck began to ache from arching it backward so she let her head relax forward as her fingers continued the cat-and-mouse game with the elusive canister. Perspiration combined with the water on her hands made the task about as easy as catching a slippery eel with one greased finger. Her leg and back muscles tightened in agony. Her cheeks flushed from exertion. She wanted to curse the canister taunting her just beyond her grasp.

"Would you like some help now?"

"No." She heard his laughter bubbling its way to

the surface. She was dying to say yes, but she railed at the chauvinist motivation behind his offer. She squashed the small voice whispering to her that she was being foolish. Hell would freeze over before she'd give him the satisfaction of yielding to his offer of that superior male help.

She felt her shorts inch up and cursed the fact she was giving him a private showing of too much flesh. The muscles in her arms were killing her, and if she didn't get the stupid sugar soon, she'd scream. She gave one more stretch, straining high on tiptoes.

Finally she felt the stupid canister budge. Her perspiring fingertips walked over the top of the container, tilting it slowly. . . . She knew exactly what Kipp was thinking, and she almost turned around to gloat over her victory. "Aaah, here it comes." Then in a flash, victory changed to horror as the canister took on a life of its own. Her sweaty hands couldn't grab the slippery cylinder. It tilted drunkenly and hung precariously at the edge of the shelf, before it decided which route to take before plunging. Kipp moved, but he wasn't fast enough to head off disaster.

"Stop!" Stacy screamed uselessly as the August summer disappeared under a January snowstorm . . . five pounds of cane sugar slaloming over the edge of the shelf. In seconds the white avalanche lay in heaps and trails, clumping and pooling in crazy designs on different parts of her body.

"Dammit. I don't need this!" Her arms flailed wildly.

Nothing was spared. What wasn't on the outside of her clothing found a gritty nest in her bra, the valley between her breasts, her navel, and under the elastic band of her bikini panties. Like dry shampoo, white granules streaked and settled in her hair. The spaces between her toes looked as if she were at the beach. Then she became aware of a chortle in back of her and she swirled around.

"You're tall. Why didn't you help me?" She spat sugar with her accusation as her white-flecked eyelashes batted in anger. It didn't matter that she had flatly refused his help not once, but twice. A real gentleman wouldn't have asked.

Kipp was slapping his hands against his thighs and shaking his head. He couldn't resist it. "You're . . ."

She glared. "What?"

"Sweet." He doubled up laughing. "Now I know what the sugar plum fairy looks like."

It was the wrong thing to say. She took a swipe at the hands trying to steady her and had the satisfaction of seeing him sprinkled with sugar too.

"Wait a minute."

"What for?" she snapped.

Engulfed in laughter, he wiped the tears from his eyes, then put a restraining hand on her shoulder. He grabbed his empty cup, hastily scooping it into a mound of sugar on the counter.

"Waste not, want not," he said and wagged his eyebrows in a fairly good imitation of Groucho Marx.

That was the last straw for Stacy. Her brave front collapsed. She brushed her hand across her face, biting her lip to hold back the tears forming in her eyes. Instantly Kipp's mood changed.

"Look, I'm sorry," he said. "Let me help clean up this mess. I'm the one who's obviously causing you to come apart at the seams."

She didn't want his help. She was itchy. She wanted to crawl upstairs and shower before becoming a walking ant farm. Her shoulders sagged in defeat and her chin fell against her chest. Kipp put his finger under her chin and lifted it to look full into her face.

"Okay?" His voice was gentle and soothing.

Mutely she nodded as grains of sugar wafted down

to the floor. There was nothing she could do to deter him anyhow. She had the distinct feeling his wife, Millie, couldn't control him any better than she had, that indeed no one could control this irrespressible hunk.

Kipp set about the task of brushing her off, holding her still with one hand while the other expertly skimmed over her bare arms and legs.

As his hands started to brush the sugar from the front of her shirt, she stiffened. "I'll get that."

"Hey, it's all right. I don't bite. Come over to the sink. Let's get it out of your hair."

She was giving him every reason, she thought, to believe that her brains would disappear down the drain with the sugar. The sooner she let him do the noble thing, the faster she'd get rid of him. Nodding agreement, she leaned her head over the stainless steel basin, giving Kipp a view of the nape of her neck.

She was anchored firmly between the sink and rock-hard stomach muscles, firm thighs, and muscular legs. Tilting her head to the side, she saw the fine sheen of dark hair on Kipp's sinewy arms. There was no escape, not from the feel of him or from the warm breath sending shivers down her spine.

"Relax, I'm really quite good at this."

I'll bet, she thought.

One of Stacy's greatest joys was to have her back rubbed. With the motion of Kipp's fingers riffling through her hair, she dropped her head forward, drifting along on the sensuous waves of pleasure. Over and over, gentle fingers massaged her head. The fingers moved downward along the column of her neck to her stiff shoulder muscles. A soft sigh escaped her lips and reached upward to the ear of the man whose loins responded to the rounded derriere tucked in front of him.

Her eyelids drifted shut. In the days and nights she had spent alone, Stacy had wondered how she would react to a man's touch. Now she knew. Much to her surprise, this stranger with twinkling blue eyes, who smelled of lemony soap, whose voice could tease or soothe like melting butter, this bold, audacious giant of a man married to a woman named Millie was causing a stirring in the pit of her stomach. The thought was terrifying! And it snapped her right out of her reverie.

"That's enough."

"What, no thanks?"

"Thanks." Why did he make her feel that she was a guest in her own kitchen?

"Here, sit down." He pushed her unceremoniously into the nearest chair, disregarding her feeble protests. "Where's your dustpan?"

Avoiding his face, she pointed to the utility closet near the cellar door, grateful for the distance.

"Then next time I go shopping," he said matter-of-factly, "I'll replace this stuff."

"No need."

"I insist. And by the way, you have a very nice place here," he said, making her wonder why he was changing the subject.

The kitchen was bright, with splashes of yellow and orange flowers on the papered walls. Potted asparagus ferns perched on a ledge in front of the double windows over the sink, beyond which was the spacious yard. Gleaming copper pans hung from an arced wrought iron rack near the double oven. It was a cheerful room, one in which Stacy loved to work or sit quietly at the butcher-block table beneath the high leaded bay windows, sipping a second cup of coffee while reading the local newspaper.

"There, that's the last of it," Kipp announced as

he emptied the contents of the dustpan into the garbage. He beckoned to her, "Come outside and I'll hose you off."

The man never gave up! Did he really expect her to allow him to get that personal again? She could just imagine her wet clothes clinging to her body.

"Never mind. As soon as you leave, I'm going up to shower."

"Suit yourself," he said.

Her instinct was to bolt past him. Instead, she escorted him to the patio, pretending there wasn't any more sugar hiding in crevices of her body.

There was one more thing left to do to make certain he'd have no reason to pop in on her again. Summoning a false cheery voice, she said, "Tell your wife not to return the sugar. Call it a welcome-to-the-neighborhood gift."

He gazed at her for a long moment. When his hand reached up to brush off some sugar that clung to her shoulder, she had the craziest desire to turn her head into his open palm, but she held herself to her rigid pose. Why did she have the weird feeling that the message she directed to his wife somehow displeased him?

His knuckles briefly touched her cheek. "Thanks."

She admired his long lazy strides that ate up the distance to the stockade gate. He turned, and she thought for a moment he'd forgotten something.

"I really think a more gentle touch is called for with those roses," he said gravely. "You'd be surprised what you can get with honey instead of vinegar. Or should I have said sugar?"

Two

A squeaky-clean Stacy flopped across her bed and stared at the ceiling. What was she going to do? How was she going to cover her tracks? She'd be damned if she was going to run away and hide every weekend!

Twisting her thin gold wedding band, she gnashed her teeth, remembering the day she proudly held up her hand to the light to show Bev the modest diamond engagement ring, her heart brimming with love. "Harry is everything." It was her benediction to him, intoned in all seriousness.

"No man is everything, kiddo," Bev had declared in her flat nasal tones. "Brush the stars out of your eyes and give yourself a chance to date other guys."

Maybe if she'd followed her friend's advice she wouldn't be staring at the ceiling trying to figure a way out of the lies she had told just over an hour ago to her new neighbor. The last thing she needed was to have Kipp Palmer check up on her. She flipped over on the king-size bed that was acres too large for one person and considered her options.

She could move.

Ridiculous.

She could tell the truth.

Absolutely not!

She could figure out a way to trick Mr. Sexy Blue Eyes.

Definitely.

In fact, after the rotten way he'd amused himself at her expense, it would serve the louse right!

Her brain whirled like a computer processing and spitting out useless information. Garbage in, garbage out. It went on like that until a tiny germ of an idea seeded and put out roots. The more she thought about it, the more she liked it, and for the first time in hours a smile spread across her face, lighting up her hazel eyes.

Sir Walter Scott's famous quote from *Marmion* looped around in her head like a broken record.

> Oh, what a tangled web we weave,
> When first we practice to deceive!

Abruptly she rose from the bed, knowing the aphids and the slugs were merrily eating their way through her flowers and vegetables.

First things first, Kipp Palmer.

"But soon, my nosy neighbor," she whispered, "you'll learn that two can play at this game!"

Kipp placed the measuring cup on the crowded yellow ceramic-tiled countertop in his kitchen. A whisk, a garlic press, a lemon squeezer, a shrimp deveiner, an apple corer, a butter slicer, a rind remover that resembled a crochet hook, and other utensils he had no intention of using waited to be put in drawers once the lining paper was in. They were housewarming gifts from his twin sister, Millie, who was helping him get settled.

"Here's the sugar," Kipp said.

Millie returned his smile and gestured to the boxes piled up against the wall. "Frank and I were wondering why you didn't rent an apartment. Do you think it's wise with your schedule to tie yourself down to a house? Especially now?"

He knew his sister and brother-in-law had his best interests at heart. So he answered honestly and simply. "It seemed the right time for a change of lifestyle. Felicia never wanted a house. I did. After our divorce last year, I decided when the lease was up on the apartment to rent a house and see what I was missing. If I like the area, I'll look around for a house to buy." He neglected to add the neighborhood already provided a most compelling diversion: a small blonde package with a feisty mind of her own.

Millie cut into his memories. "What's your neighbor like?" she asked.

"She's all right," he said, giving away nothing. "When I told her you wanted the sugar, she assumed you were my wife."

"I'm glad you straightened her out."

"I didn't." He grinned, the corners of his eyes crinkling in boyish mischief.

"Are you crazy?" Millie demanded. "Why not?"

"Stop worrying," he said, immediately sorry for opening his mouth. "I'm going to be here for only a year. Besides, I've thought it all out." That wasn't exactly true. He wasn't really sure what perverse pleasure had kept him from correcting Stacy's misconception, but, he reasoned, it wouldn't be the first time in recorded history the price of freedom carried a share of deception. At any rate, a cup of sugar, or in this case five pounds of it, hardly deserved the trading of life stories.

"Go ahead," Millie said, wiping her hands on the towel and giving him her full attention. "Explain to me how Phi Beta Kappa who goes on to get an M.D. reasons. I'm dying to hear this."

It was too late to escape Millie's dry wit. "I'm sick and tired of well-meaning people trying to fix me up. I get enough of that sort of thing at the hospital. This may sound egotistical, but women play subtle games, especially with doctors. The minute they know I'm single they dangle a list of names of available women in front of me. You'd think it's a crime not to be married."

"You're right." Millie gestured with a spatula coated with chocolate batter. "It does sound egotistical. And damned unfair too. Just remember, you men have the numbers in your favor."

"Oh, come off your feminist pedestal. All I'm saying is on my home turf I don't want to be annoyed. I'd just as soon the neighbors know as little as possible about my personal life. It isn't as if I intend to socialize with them."

"Maybe not, but how are you going to explain my extended absence to your next-door neighbor?"

"Simple," he said, crossing his fingers behind his back. "I'm not. Why should I? What could happen? There's little chance of our paths crossing again."

His sister's cerulean blue eyes were the same shade as Kipp's, but they weren't amused. "I still think your short excursion in the sun addled your brain."

"For just a year it's no big deal," he grumbled, feeling the pressure of her logic. From long experience he knew once Millie made a point she considered valid, she didn't let go.

But to his surprise she did this time. Millie's sudden flare-up of temper vanished like the tail of a comet. "I know you've been burned and I'd like to strangle Felicia for the piranha she turned out to be—"

"But?"

"Nothing, far be it from me to preach. You've made your bed and you can lie in it. Figuratively speaking, of course. I wouldn't recommend a liaison with a married woman, especially if she's a neighbor with time on her hands."

"You always were a worrywart."

"With good reason. You've been out of commission by choice for too long. I think it's crazy for you to be a recluse. From the predatory gleam in your eye when you came in from the good neighbor's house, I'd say it's time you began to date again. I'd be happy to introduce you to some nice unmarried women," she added pointedly.

He started to protest, but she kept right on speaking. "Whether you know it or not, your juices are flowing. Anyway, dear brother, I wish you luck. Something tells me you're going to need it. I'm just sorry I can't be a fly on the wall when she learns the truth!"

Kipp swatted his twin's trim behind. An affectionate smile passed between them. They had been playing mind-reading games since childhood with uncanny accuracy. He loved his pain-in-the-neck sister with the special bonding of twins, but this time she was dead wrong. No way would he allow himself to become entangled with a married woman no matter how much his juices flowed!

"I think she's upset about something," he said offhandedly as he peered into the mixing bowl.

"What makes you think so?" she repeated.

Kipp ran his little finger around the rim of the

mixing bowl and scooped up a taste of the chocolate batter before his sister rapped his knuckles.

"What makes you think so?" she repeated.

"For openers, she's jumpy as hell." A look of amazement came over his features. "Can you believe it? She actually slammed the door in my face."

His sense of wonder almost made Millie laugh. Then her feminine intuition took over. "Describe her for me," Millie said.

The faint lines around Kipp's eyes wrinkled in pleasure. Vibrant colors intertwined in his brain, spinning out shades of tawny golden hair and creamy skin, engagingly piquant brows, delicate earlobes, and lips that were adorable even when she pouted. He remembered her hazel eyes flecked with gold and sooty lashes tipped in copper that dared him not to laugh as she tugged at the hem of her brief shorts . . . shorts that accentuated long, graceful legs, inciting his senses to imagine other things.

"She's okay, I guess," Kipp said at last.

"That's it?" Millie sounded disappointed.

"What more should there be? She's young, somewhere on the upper range of twenty. Her husband racks up air mileage with some kind of a job that keeps him on the go. I didn't see any evidence of children underfoot."

Millie placed the cake in the oven and set the timer. "You gleaned quite a bit of information while borrowing just a cup of sugar."

Kipp knew she was baiting him. "Stop trying to make something out of nothing. Go home. You've been wonderful and I appreciate it. Give Frank my best and stop worrying. Everything will be all right. Besides, I'll be picking up Connie tomorrow. He'll keep me company."

"You call that Great Dane company? More like a

garbage pail with flying fur. I'll be glad to get him out of my house before he chews up all of Frank's shoes."

Millie ducked under Kipp's arm, gave him an affectionate squeeze, and said, "I'm going now, you're all set. Please, give what I said some thought."

After seeing Millie out, Kipp went upstairs to his room. He unpacked his high-powered telescope and carefully mounted it on its tripod base. He placed it near the window, focused the lens, and tested the scope at several ranges. Tonight the forecast indicated clear northern skies, and Kipp was looking forward to stargazing.

As if controlled by another hand, the scope swooped downward at a right angle, aiming itself directly at the house opposite his. The sun streamed through the window, backlighting the room. He didn't need a map to tell him where he was.

Stacy's bedroom—sharply clear, tantalizingly close, and completely feminine—was at his eye level. He felt as if he could reach out and touch the bed in which she slept. It was king-size and covered by a white eyelet bedspread. He laughed aloud at the two stuffed animals on the pillows. Kermit the Frog nestled in the paws of an enormous Pooh bear outfitted in a Scotsman's beret and kilt.

His gaze slid to a small fluff of pale pink lingerie near the foot of the bed. Kipp recognized it as a teddy. He allowed himself the pleasurable image of Stacy inching a spaghetti strap over her shoulder as her gold-flecked eyes beckoned him with a come-hither look. He sighed heavily and swung the scope toward the backyard. Stacy was once more toiling in the hot sun. Skimpily dressed in a halter top and shorts, she seemed oblivious to the need to protect herself. Knowing what he did about the dangers of ultraviolet rays on the skin and especially on her delicate Nordic coloring, he felt like going down there and lathering her with number fifteen suntan lotion. Then he'd shove a hat on her head and gloves on her hands.

The scope brought her so close he could almost reach out and kiss the pulse point at the base of her throat. Like a flower unfurling its petals, Stacy began to straighten up from her cramped position. With tantalizing slowness she arced her arms high above her ponytailed head. His breath quickened as she treated him to an enticing view of her breasts.

When she slowly stood up, he traced the graceful line of her thighs to her smooth calf and down to her shapely ankles. Then his lips curved in a wide smile as his eyes swept over her feet.

He discovered a secret.

Stacy Conklin's vanity was showing.

Poking out of a pair of red leather thongs, ten dainty red-tipped toenails informed him that his neighbor did think about things other than gardening. He could imagine her leaning over a bended leg, dabbing polish on each toe, then blowing on them to speed the drying process. Frowning at the glare of the hot sun, he shook his head in despair. What a pity to damage such delicate skin! Still, she was no kid, and he really couldn't tell her what to do.

"Little fool," he muttered, watching Stacy wipe her forehead. The woman simply refused to be sensible. Mad dogs, Englishmen, and Stacy Conklin venture out in the noonday sun, he thought. Not only did she venture out. She stayed out!

Throwing caution to the winds, he flung open the window with such force the panes rattled in their casings.

"Get out of the damn sun! Or wear a hat and

gloves!" he bellowed, driven to frustration by his concern for her. With some satisfaction he saw his warning hit home.

A stunned look came over her face. Her mouth formed a perfect O. Her ponytail whipped through the air as her head snapped up to find him. A hand shaded the sun from her eyes. For a few long seconds they stared wordlessly at each other. Then a very unladylike epithet sailed through the air, stinging his ears as Stacy flung the trowel from her hand. It landed with a loud clang on the patio. For the second time in one day Kipp heard the loud reverberations of a door being slammed.

Steaming mad and sizzling at the boiling point, Stacy rushed into the house. Her heart pounded in her ears; her mouth felt like fuzz balls. She blew on the blisters on her palms to lessen the sting. She wanted to break something but knew she'd have to clean it up if she did.

She settled for a cold drink of lemonade.

Wincing from sore hands, she carefully removed the pitcher from the refrigerator. She poured herself a tall glassful and gulped it down. It was pure bliss. She refilled her glass a second time.

Then she allowed herself to think about *him*!

She knew very well she'd been out in the sun too long and that Kipp's warning was meant for her benefit. But still, he had *yelled* at her, loud enough to alert all the busybodies in the neighborhood.

She moaned as she pursed her lips to blow on her hands again. Why wasn't he at work on a Wednesday afternoon rather than at home wearing nothing but tight pants and a medallion around his neck? He was handsome, she had to admit, and he might very well be the second sexiest man she'd ever seen, but so what? Even if he weren't married, she wanted nothing to do with him. Not with her track record.

She removed the Essex County phone directory from the shelf above her desk and flipped through the yellow pages until she located the number she needed.

It was time to set her plan in motion!

Three

Rick Samuels, proprietor, professional photographer, and president of the Englewood, New Jersey, Chamber of Commerce, according to the embossed business card Stacy nervously bent in her blistered hand, carefully flicked a piece of lint from the sleeve of his madras shirt. Except for her, the Village Camera Shop was devoid of customers. It was just as well. Stacy was certain she looked as dumbfounded as she felt.

"I was under the impression, Mrs. Conklin, that you represented a business firm. When we spoke, you never indicated you wanted only one picture. That's why it's so expensive."

"I'm sorry," she said in a low, strained voice. "I thought I made that clear on the phone this morning."

"No, unfortunately, you didn't," he said, sure of his memory. "It's a set fee. The price for what you're asking is two hundred fifty dollars."

Stacy mentally counted the money left in her meager bank account. Living on a rapidly diminishing summer budget, she knew it would be weeks before she could replenish her funds.

"Would you care to think about it?" he asked, sensing her distress.

Think about it? She wished she could forget about it. But, after Kipp Palmer's cavalier intrusion into her life, the need to keep him securely on his side of the fence was more important than ever. Not only didn't he take no for an answer this morning, but later, after she resumed her gardening, she actually caught him spying on her from his upstairs window.

Stacy closed her eyes for a moment and drew a deep decisive breath. Drastic problems required drastic measures!

"No." She forced herself to speak calmly. "It's just that I didn't understand what's involved in blowing up a picture to a life-size portrait and mounting it on cardboard."

Rick Samuels ducked his head under the counter for a moment. A pudgy hand grabbed a blue looseleaf book with large gold-leafed letters on the front and spine. "What you want is what we call display photography." He laid the book on the glass counter and swiveled it toward Stacy.

There were colored life-size replicas of Prince Philip, President Reagan, Dolly Parton, and Clint Eastwood. The blisters on her hand were making it difficult to turn the pages. "But I thought all you did was blow up a picture to life size and mount it on cardboard." How much could cardboard cost?

"If you wanted the picture mass produced, it would probably cost twenty dollars per item. However, you're asking for only one. There's a lot involved. First, we need to shoot a new picture from an old picture to get it on thirty-five millimeter film. That gives us a negative to work with. Then we mount the picture on heavy corrugated cardboard. Finally, and it's tricky, we hand-cut it. Unless you want it on plastic?" His gray eyes peered at her above his half glasses with a hopeful expression.

"No." She swallowed hard. She didn't want to ruffle his feathers after she was lucky enough to find him. Samuels was the only photographer for miles around who did this specialized work. And, she fumed inwardly, if it weren't for her neighbor who couldn't mind his own damn business, she wouldn't be here.

Rick Samuels picked up his explanation where he left off. "As I was saying, mass production is different. Then we die-cut. It's cheaper. Are you sure you can't use one hundred?"

One hundred cardboard Harrys peeping out the windows? She laughed in spite of herself. "One is all I need."

"Do you want him to move?" Stacy looked at him quizzically. "Move. You know, move his arms up and down. If so, we put grommets at the joints." The photographer demonstrated the puppetlike movements as he spoke.

"How much is that?" she asked. What the hell, if she could make Harry thumb his nose at the busybody who was giving her all this trouble, she would.

"Not that much. You're spending this much. What's a few dollars more?"

Groceries, she thought glumly, tallying up all the pasta dinners in her future. "All right. Grommets."

"How about a motor?"

"A motor?" What was Harry going to do? Follow her around like a puppy?"

"Haven't you ever seen a display in a drugstore that moves in place?" Twirling his finger, he imitated the ballerina on the glass counter. "You know, goes round and round. There's a nine-volt battery in back of it." He leaned forward, pencil in hand, ready to write.

Stacy couldn't resist. "How much for the motor?"

"Motion display," he corrected her tapping his pencil on the looseleaf book. "To buy only one is about eighteen dollars. If you buy in bulk, they're about three dollars apiece."

"No motor." Harry going round and round like a merry-go-round was too much. All she could think of was a carnival booth. She'd probably be tempted to throw balls at him to win a prize.

Stacy signed the order and gritted her teeth as she wrote a check for a larger amount than she had planned.

"We'll do a nice job for you," Samuels said, trying to soften the blow of the high cost. "You'll receive a call from us in about eight or nine days so you can pick it up."

Her eyes widened; her mouth dropped open. She completely overlooked the obvious. Harry couldn't sit. In his stiffened condition all he could do was lay down, and even for that her car wasn't long enough. "Oh, dear, I'm afraid my automobile isn't large enough. Do you deliver?"

"No problem. We can deliver it."

Smiling, she let out a sigh of relief until she remembered another crucial fact. For her scheme to work, Harry's homecoming must be secret! "And would you please deliver at night? I work during the day."

"How about leaving it with your neighbor?"

"No." The word came out much more sharply than she planned. "My neighbors are elderly, sick people," she lied. "I never bother them."

Rick Samuels flipped the pages on a desk calendar and made a notation to deliver the Conklin order.

By the time Stacy turned the ignition key in her automobile and steered her car into the traffic lane, she was feeling pretty smug. So far, so good.

She hummed gleefully. If she positioned Cardboard Harry behind the sheer curtains in her bedroom, it would convince Kipp, his wife, anyone, that her "husband" was home.

She slipped a Sinatra cassette into the tape deck and listened dreamily to his sexy intonation of "I've Got You Under My Skin." In a wild and wacky way she drew a connection between the title of the song and Kipp Palmer's calamitous effect on her life. Like the words in the song, her disturbing new neighbor with his magnetic blue eyes certainly succeeded in getting under her skin.

More than once!

The clincher that had brought her to the Village Camera Shop happened after the second incident with her new neighbor. She numbered those incidents like wars. First the Sugar Incident, then the Spying Incident. She bristled as she recalled the circumstances. It had happened so suddenly, it literally took away her breath. One minute she was busily pruning and fertilizing her comatose plants, the next minute, right out of the blue, she was being screamed at. Without the slightest warning Kipp had flung open his window and delivered a thunderous reprimand to her about how she was dressed for the sun.

He should talk! Framed in the window, all six feet plus of him, hands braced against his lean hips, long legs wide apart in a buccaneer's stance, he was clad only in a pair of tight-fitting pants outlining the muscles in his thighs like a second skin. Twinkling against his bare chest, taunting her, a gold medallion caught the sun's rays and blinked its special brand of Morse code.

She couldn't even yell back. By the time she gathered her wits, the big lug had disappeared just like that! Poof. Curtain down. End of Act One.

She drove faster than the speed limit, and gave in to the urge to scream, much to the surprise of the driver in the car pacing hers in the other lane. A wellspring of untapped righteous indignation rose in her chest. In one day Kipp Palmer shattered the calm of what used to be a serenely quiet life on a serenely quiet street.

An exhausted Stacy tumbled wearily into bed, looking forward to the first peaceful night's sleep in a long time.

It lasted until exactly two A.M., when for the fifth time in as many nights the sound of a garage door squeaking along its rusty metal track penetrated her sleep-fogged state.

"Not again, dammit!" She was off the bed in a flash. "Ouch!" Her little toe caught the edge of a sharp metal point which punctured the skin deeply. The pain shot up her foot, exploding before her eyes. She spewed unladylike curses equally to her neighbor and the gunmetal-gray file case she had forgotten to replace on her desk. The vitriolic name-calling reverberated off the walls in the stiflingly close room, floating out the open window to lay heavily in the humid air outside.

Tears of frustration and pain welled up in her eyes as she hobbled toward the window. The dank, oppressively humid air hung heavy for the fifth straight night. Trees and bushes drooped low on their branches; moisture belled on the windowsill.

The sounds of the night were stifled by cicadas whirring their large transparent wings noisily. An occasional bright flash of a firefly sent tiny light charges slicing through the still darkness.

Stacy's sheer cotton gown was plastered to her body. Beads of perspiration trickled down her neck and between her breasts. Wiping her damp forehead with the back of her hand, she couldn't remember feeling more clammy . . . or miserable.

It was too much to bear. "Kipp Palmer," she railed into the night, "oil that stupid garage door! You don't have the right to cat around in the middle of the night waking me up, for Pete's sake!" Everything was his fault. How could her luck be so rotten?

Sniffling back the tears, she swiveled on her good heel and aimed for the bed. The dark distorted her judgment, images shifting in barely reflected moonlight. Losing her balance, she almost missed the edge of the mattress and yelped as the palms of her hands slid along the top sheet.

Her shoulders slumped forward as she sat dejectedly on the bed. Under stress, Stacy sometimes developed migraine headaches. From the throbbing in her temples she recognized the beginnings of a whopping one, which, she knew from experience, would get a lot worse before it got better. She took deep even breaths and tried to disregard the pounding in her head. As she sat there shaking, she heard another noise vying for her attention, and it didn't originate beneath her scalp.

"Oh, no!" she wailed. The rapping of knuckles became more and more insistent. Then Stacy heard her name called repeatedly in tones somewhere between hoarse whispers and shouts. "Go away," she said over and over, but she knew he wouldn't just fade away. Not Kipp!

With a resigned sigh she realized she'd have to go down and face him. She certainly wasn't going to engage in a screaming match and take the chance of alerting the whole neighborhood.

Wishing for a magic carpet to transport her injured foot and her aching head downstairs, she resigned herself to reality and carefully inched her way off the bed. When she applied pressure to her foot, stars danced in front of her eyes. She paused only long enough to allow the worst of the throbbing to settle down and then tried again, hopping and hobbling until she reached the landing.

In the dim reflected light the staircase loomed eerily and presented a challenge equal to descending the steps of the Great Wall of China. While she considered her options, the rapping on the door became louder and louder.

"Hold your horses!" she cried out, then clamped her mouth shut, remembering it was the middle of the night.

Groping for the security of the oak banister at the top of the landing, she plopped down on her rump and slowly bounced her way down the stairs. Muttering her disgust with Kipp over his nocturnal habits, she vowed to tell him in no uncertain terms exactly what she thought of his selfish, arrogant manner. If he went home to complain to his wife, tough!

The narrow hallway leading to the rear door housed Stacy's washer and dryer. A wooden hat rack filled with old gardening shirts and straw hats hung on the wall opposite the appliances. As she hobbled through the tiny area, a disturbing beam of light shone directly into her eyes, forcing her to toss her head to the side. Protectively, she threw her hands up in front of her eyes to escape its glare.

"Quit doing that," she hissed, opening the door only wide enough to make herself heard. What she intended to say could be communicated through the crack.

One large foot firmly wedged itself between the small crevice and the doorframe. Off balance she was no match for the large, determined shoe wiggling an entrance to her house. Soon the foot was followed by a leg and body. When Kipp angled his broad shoulder into the passageway, she was forced to step backward. The edge of the washing machine jammed against her spine. It felt like a gun at her back. There was no escape. Less than twelve inches separated them. He showed no signs of moving, and she couldn't.

Her heart beat erratically as she realized her dilemma. Twenty-four hours ago her life was predictably lousy but there was hope for the future. Now, here she was, in the middle of the night, with literally nowhere to move, trapped by a total stranger who behaved erratically. Worse still, if someone happened to be peering in the window, Kipp completely dwarfed her. A rash of recent robberies filled the newspapers with ghastly stories of women foolish enough to open their doors to strangers or chance acquaintances. Menacingly, he fit both categories. The folly of her actions gripped her and her knees began to shake.

"Are you all right?" Dispensing with preliminaries, Kipp shut the door behind him and she gasped.

She needn't have worried. Whatever wild notions she entertained about being ravaged flew out the window. His brusquely asked question shattered the remnants of her active imagination, bringing an instant retort.

"Do I look all right?" she snapped, piqued at him

and herself for the vivid scenes in her fertile mind. She glared at him waiting for his answer.

The waspish tone in her voice settled one thing for Kipp—he knew there was no immediate danger. His intense blue eyes regarded her steadily, openly, and to her furious discomfort a devilish twinkle appeared in them. His eyes roved the outline of her slim figure illuminated by his flashlight's beam. The nipples of her breasts thrust proudly against the scooped bodice of her pale blue nightgown, trapping his gaze and quickening his breath.

Her heart drummed furiously in her chest. He looked exactly like a man judging flesh. Hers! "Turn that thing off. You shouldn't even be here. Why were you banging at my door?"

"You haven't answered my question." He dragged his eyes back to her face and noticed for the first time that her lower lip was quite lusciously full, even a little pouty. Her pink tongue darted out to lick nervously at the corner of her mouth. Intrigued by the simple nervous action, he wished she'd do it again.

She felt a flush of embarrassment suffuse her face. It was too late. Intent on spewing out her anger, she had foolishly neglected to put on her robe. Once again with him she was dressed skimpily. Only this time he wasn't screaming at her to cover up! No. This time his lips quirked in a ready laugh.

She bit her bottom lip and swallowed a lump of humiliation. Frantically her eyes darted to a batiste shirt hanging on the hat rack. She thrust out her arm to reach beyond him, immediately checked the rash motion but thudded backward into the washing machine.

Against his baser instincts and struggling to maintain an outward calmness, Kipp acted chivalrously.

"Here," he said, covering his amusement with a high degree of pretended gravity. "I believe I'm preventing you from reaching your shirt."

He didn't fool her for a minute! Stacy yanked the shirt from his hands. Diving her arms through the sleeves, she pulled the front tails together, the blisters on her palms hurting.

"What the—? Let me see your hands!" he demanded.

She shook her head, a froth of blonde ringlets bouncing around her face. But Kipp Palmer was not a man to be denied. Swiftly he grabbed her wrists and turned the palms over for inspection. "Hold still, for goodness' sake. I'm not going to hurt you." He saw what he expected to see; the warning he'd yelled out the window had come much too late. Raw skin festered in the middle of each palm. He muttered an oath. In an oblique reference to his earlier admonition, he said tersely, "You should have worn gloves."

She tried to pull her hands loose from his grasp, but his strength although gentle was firm. "Just go," she said.

"Don't be silly," he said gruffly. "You're hurt. I heard you scream. What happened to you? You gave me quite a scare. I know you're alone here. The least I could do is show off my good neighbor policy."

"Are you really so obtuse?" she asked irritably, irked by his questions and his insufferable gallantry when the cause of her problems was standing right in front of her too blind to see the nose in front of his face. Besides, if anyone had the right to demand answers, it was she.

"Listen, you keep crazy hours, but that's your business. However, I do wish you'd oil your damn garage door track. It's awakened me every night since you moved in." She didn't have to add that the neighborhood used to be a nice quiet place. It was in the tone of her voice.

"I'm sorry," he said matter-of-factly. "There's nothing I can do for past indiscretions, but—"he glanced fixedly at the palms of her hands—"the least I can do is treat those blisters." He smiled impishly.

"Tell you what, if you oil those runners, I'll forgive you." Tilting off balance, she grimaced in pain and hid her foot with its bleeding toe by tucking it behind her leg. It probably made her look like a flamingo, she thought.

For the first time Kipp noticed the small raised foot with the red toenails pointed downward. A thin trail of blood trickled down the side. "Why didn't you tell me you injured your foot?"

He didn't wait for an answer. She found herself lifted, wrapped securely in strong arms, braced against a muscular chest, and carried into the kitchen. At the entrance he paused momentarily to locate the switch plate, moved his hand to flood the room with light, strode over to the butcher-block table, hooked his shoe around the leg of a chair, dragging it away from the table, and seated her. Before she could protest his Tarzan routine, he asked brusquely, "Where do you keep your supplies?"

"Supplies?"

"Bandages, antiseptics, you know, first aid supplies. Every house has them." He sounded exasperated, and she knew he'd like her answer even less.

"I'm afraid I ran out." His arched brow told her she was right.

"Wait here."

She heard him say something under his breath that had to do with his opinion of her. At least she was grateful he had the presence of mind to close the screen door quietly. Rattled by his supercilious attitude, she decided he must be comparing Millie's efficiency to her lack of it.

When he returned shortly, he was all business. "All right, . . ." he said. "Let's attend to these hands of yours." He made a grunting sound of disapproval when he saw the full extent of her blisters, turned his back to her, and busied himself laying out his first aid equipment. "I have to clean this first."

"I can do it myself."

"You're the most obstinate female I've ever met. Do you always go around trying to prove you're superwoman? Now, hold still and let me do this."

"Well," she said defensively, "you weren't going out in the middle of the night to bandage a hand, now, were you?" She was amazed at her audacity.

"Hardly. I'm a doctor and you're being ornery." His blue eyes glittered mischievously. "Why else would I be sneaking around in the middle of the night?" The smug look on his face told her he had heard the oaths shouted into the darkness. "That was the general idea of your message, wasn't it?"

Her lower jaw dropped open. He lifted a finger to her chin and closed her lips. She knew her cheeks must be blazing.

"Frankly," she said, sounding suspicious in the face of such nobility, "I didn't think doctors made house calls anymore."

"Some do." Shrugging his shoulders, he raised his head and looked her full in the eye. He held up a bottle of Zephrian. "This has a water base; it won't sting the way alcohol does. All you'll feel is the coolness of the liquid." Paying no attention to her meager protest, he poured the antiseptic on a gauze square and dabbed gently at her wounds. Using a tweezer, he worked quickly to remove bits of dangling loose skin. Then he applied a yellowish salve and covered the area with a sterile bandage.

"Feel better?"

She had to admit the soothing ointment and not having the blisters exposed to the air made her hands ache less. "They really do. Look, I don't want to keep you—"

"Suppose you let me decide where I want to be." His eyes smiled into hers and the room seemed brighter. She squiggled back on the chair and sighed. It felt so good to have someone take care of her, however briefly. "Oh, wait, there's a footstool in the living room by the rocker. Wouldn't that be easier for you?"

"Good idea." He returned with the footstool and sat down, extending his long legs on either side of Stacy's chair. Then he lifted her foot and rested it on his leg. She noticed again his long, tapered fingers and his immaculately groomed fingernails. He tested for broken bones around her ankle, felt the puffy skin on top of her foot, then turned it to better see the gash at the base of her toenail. "I'm going to clean this out, then I'll be able to tell if it needs a stitch. It's pretty deep."

"A stitch?" Her voice trembled. Although half the boys in her classes regularly got stitched up for something or other, the thought frightened her. "What kind of a doctor are you?"

"I'm a surgeon." Her vivid imagination saw shiny knives gleaming in neat rows. He sat back and held her foot as if it belonged to him and not to her. "I'm eminently qualified to treat something as simple as this."

She pictured the needle being threaded. "I shouldn't be keeping you. Your patient . . ."

"Is probably sleeping."

"Then why were you . . .?"

"Going out? I hate to disappoint you about my nightly jaunts, but there's a child in the hospital I operated on. Until he's out of danger I check on him often."

"Oh . . . oh, then you were on your way to . . . and I . . ." The man was trying to get to the hospital in the middle of the night to visit a seriously ill child while she screeched out the window doing a banshee imitation. On top of that he realized she was afraid of stitches. No wonder he'd been amused! She digested the new ideas. Not many doctors today cared so much about their patients. She pulled her foot out of his hand. It landed painfully on the floor.

"Millie will worry if you're gone too long."

"I doubt that. Now be good," he said, "and let me finish." Unceremoniously, he picked her foot up again, placing it this time in the small space on the footstool where his thighs joined. Stacy gulped. She kept her toes at right angles to the ceiling while he acted as if it were the most natural place in the world for her foot to be.

"You know"—his hand caressed her foot and he looked her straight in the eye, "if you were my wife, I'd probably prevent you from gardening because it's injurious to your health."

He should only know it's not my favorite pastime, she mused. His light bantering only increased her predicament. As he spoke, he calmly continued his examination, holding her heel nonchalantly close to forbidden territory. That took her mind off the possibility of a stitch and got her thinking of a problem of a more immediate nature. She wondered if her loud heartbeat could be felt by his fingers.

He certainly was doing a thorough examination. Too thorough, she decided, observing him warily as he tested the skin and the fine bones of her toe, the puffy area near her ankle, and even her instep. The heat in her body increased in direct ratio to the length of time he kept her foot firmly in front of the zipper of his pants.

She tried to concentrate on other things, but his warm breath on her foot as his head inclined over it ruined her efforts. Finally, she gave up. Whatever was happening was taking place solely in her head anyway. The man in front of her was simply doing his job. It was a good thing he couldn't read her mind.

It was a good thing she couldn't read his mind, Kipp decided. His lusty thoughts were decidedly not clinical. The shirt he gave Stacy to put on over her see-through gown didn't block the memory of his first view. Twice today her nearness had set his blood racing. Nature graced Stacy with a harmony of line, form, and beauty. A dainty foot leading to a shapely leg leading to a curvaceous thigh which led to—

He knew he was taking entirely too much time bandaging her toe. He'd seen the stiffening of her body, knew exactly why she held her toes pointed toward the ceiling and could even be amused by it. He wasn't amused by his own behavior, however. If he were sitting on a medical review board judging a fellow doctor's ethical practice and the guy had acted as he was acting now, he would vote to suspend him. Millie was right: He should start dating again and stop making excuses to cozy up to his neighbor's wife.

• • •

Stacy studied the man whose broad shoulders strained the material of his open-necked sport shirt. She smelled the woodsy outdoor scent wafting from his bare skin and realized that he wasn't faithful to one scent in aftershave lotions or colognes. This morning, near the sink, she had picked up the tangy aroma of lemon.

His wrists were strong, his hands large and long, fingers tapered. He had the hands of a pianist, she thought, or the surgeon he was. Now she understood about his immaculately groomed nails, the neat half-moon cut of them, the well-tended cuticles. A sprinkling of dark hair dusted the backs of his hands, adding to his masculinity.

She wondered about how those sensitive yet strong hands would feel on her body. And suddenly she realized that "Harry's" arrival would be as much for her benefit as Kipp's.

She didn't want to think how good it had felt to snuggle against his chest, but her eyes were inexorably drawn to the dark curly hairs at the top of his T-shirt. Then her gaze rose to meet his.

They remained that way for a long moment, their eyes speaking forbidden messages. Conscious of her state of dishabille, she flustered visibly.

"You don't need a stitch," he said at last. "I was able to get by with a Steri-Strip." He folded the adhesive tape and snapped the top on the round spool.

Her shoulders shook at the absurdity of it all. Doctor or not, she wasn't his patient. He had no business behaving as if being in her house in the middle of the night were the most natural thing in the world. Not with a wife within shouting distance who was sleeping in a state of blissful ignorance.

She began to laugh, a small, rich sound rising in

an ever-increasing volume until the tears rolled silently down her cheeks. Life around him certainly wasn't dull. At every juncture thus far, his peculiar brand of aid and comfort resulted in disaster, and somehow he was making her injuries sound as if she were a mindless idiot walking into doors! First was the Sugar Incident, then the Spying Incident, and now the Garage-Door Toe-Gash Incident. If she didn't get rid of him soon, she'd be a walking Band-Aided wreck.

It was time to end this charade. She pulled her bandaged toe away. Sitting up, she tried unsuccessfully to give the impression of a stern schoolmarm.

"Thank you," she offered in her most prissy tone.

"You're welcome," replied the chastised student, his lips quivering with suppressed humor.

He gathered the first aid supplies and placed them on the counter. Without glancing in her direction, he returned the footstool to the living room. He breezed back into the kitchen, towered over the seated Stacy, and calmly threw her for another loop.

"Come on. I'll get you to bed."

"What?"

"It's going to hurt like hell if you apply pressure to your foot right now," he said.

Damn his smug attitude! Damn the whole ridiculous situation! He was right. Arguing would waste time. She nodded her head, giving him his victory.

For the second time that evening she felt him pick her up easily. She was tired, strained to the limits of her control, so she let her head loll against his chest. Once or twice she attempted to lift it and failed. It felt too good there. Finally she gave in to the feeling and let her body relax to the hard male body, to the tingling sensation of breath on her face, to feeling secure if only for a little while. Kipp tightened his arms around her small frame, glanced down at her, and smiled. Knowing she shouldn't, but with a sense of peace, she returned his smile.

At the top of the stairs he paused. Their faces were very close, and his voice was a husky whisper as he asked, "Which one?"

She pointed to her room. He carried her in, placed her on the bed with its rumpled sheets, the bed he pictured her looking so alluring in, and stepped back, knowing he should run out of there as fast as his legs could carry him.

Unconsciously he leaned forward. Stacy's heart raced. Warning bells clanged in her head. This was a doctor-patient relationship regardless of the time and place. She had to put it back on a business basis.

"Your fee?"

"My fee?" For a moment he looked thunderstruck. His hand went to the back of his neck to rub the tense knot that had suddenly developed there. What would happen if he told her his fee had already been paid? That seeing her in bed with her hair fanning the pillow was fee enough? Then, like a drowning man, his resolve flew out the window.

"Do you like anchovies?"

"Anchovies?"

"You mentioned my fee. For my sake, I'd like to see you keep out of trouble for one day. Give your toe a rest. Don't get your hands dirty, either with gardening or cooking. That means exactly what it sounds like. Of course, you won't be able to cook. Not a thing." He stared at her pointedly before resuming his orders. "I mentioned before that I believe in the good neighbor policy. Therefore, I'd appreciate it if you would share a pizza with me tonight. It'll make it a lot easier. I'm really a very busy man, Stacy. Your bandages will no doubt need changing for each of the next few days; I also have to make sure there's no infection. Now, what do you say? Will you help me save valuable time and let me kill two birds with one stone?"

What could she say? Tell him she let her imagination run away with her for the umpteenth time? She should let the poor man get on with his work. All in all it was very thoughtful of him to invite her to share a pizza with him and his wife. She supposed it was time she met Millie. She held up her hands—swaddled like a prize fighter's—and tried to shake his hand.

"If you're sure Millie won't mind, I'd love it."

"Great."

Stacy could only attribute his audible sigh of relief to her not making any further problems in his already busy schedule. Still, she felt oddly exhilarated as he said good-bye and went away whistling.

Only when she heard his car back out of his driveway did she remember that she hadn't answered his question. She didn't like anchovies on her pizza.

Four

Sometime during the night the heat wave finally broke and the temperature plummeted. Stacy drifted between waking and sleeping. She heard the birds chirping and the cars go by in the street but refused to rouse herself from blissful sleep until a cool breeze flowing steadily through the window chilled her near-naked body and brought her resentfully to full awakening. Her sheer blue nightie was bunched up around her waist. Most of the top sheet was on the floor, the rest scrunched at the foot of the bed.

She pulled down her gown and peered at her toe, wiggling it to test for pain. Thankfully, there was none. Holding up her hands in front of her face, she examined her bandages. Even her blistered palms felt better. The gauze and tape certainly proved the events of the previous evening weren't figments of her fertile imagination.

Imagine, Kipp a physician! What would he say, she wondered, if he knew she'd dreamed about him? Her pillows were jabbed so deeply they looked as if Sugar Ray had used them as punching bags. In the clear light of day her Technicolor dream wasn't only ridiculous, it was downright embarrassing, and she blushed, remembering where his hands and lips had been. She felt her pulse flutter even as she recalled their passionate embrace. But all of that was hogwash. All things considered, she was quite pleased with the way she had handled a potentially sticky situation.

Rolling onto her side, she propped herself up on her elbows and squinted out the window. There were no signs of activity at Kipp's house. Normally a light sleeper, she was surprised she hadn't heard the infernal garage door when he returned home after his visit to the hospital; she must have been sleeping very deeply. Heavens, she wondered, swinging her legs over the side of the bed, could erotic dreams act as a sleeping potion?

"Utter tripe!" She answered her own question as she stood up abruptly. It was cumbersome to walk with a toe resembling a large cotton ball, but she found she was able to bear pressure on her foot without pain and headed for the bathroom to wash.

It wasn't until after she'd said good morning to Manny and Moe, her two potted Areca palms basking under the bathroom skylight, that she noticed the note and the surgical gloves taped to the mirror over the medicine cabinet.

Stacy
Wear these.

No signature, nothing. Just two scrawled lines written in bold script. Gloves did not walk into bathrooms and attach themselves to mirrors. They needed an escort which left only one suspect, she concluded.

Kipp.

Recalling the whereabouts of the hem of her night-gown when she awoke, Stacy froze. She'd thought the pills Kipp gave her were aspirin for the pain. She racked her brain trying to think if she'd heard any noises during the night. How was she going to face him if she had treated him to a peep show? The worst part of it was she'd never know, and tonight at dinner he and Millie would be nibbling away at that pizza while she sat there mortified!

Nevertheless, she reluctantly followed Kipp's orders and slipped on the large gloves. Soaping the washcloth, she scrubbed her face until it shone. She brushed her teeth, working the bristles vigorously.

Come hell or high water, blisters or bloody toes, she swore a solemn oath: Pizza would be the last thing she'd share with Kipp. He was just too potently male, in person and in her dreams. She'd make short shrift of this evening's obligation. No return engagements, no neighborly barbecues. If by some stroke of bad fortune either Kipp or Millie suggested a get-together, she'd provide "Harry" with a convenient disease. Preferably one that couldn't be touched by Kipp's specialty, surgery, and preferably highly contagious!

Ravenous, she grabbed the first skirt and blouse she could find in her closet, dressed hurriedly and headed downstairs for the kitchen.

"What in the world—?"

She spied Kipp's second note immediately. There on the table, tied with an outrageously huge red lollipop tucked behind a red satin bow, was a bag of Dunkin' Donuts. A Spanish-language version of a Superman comic book lay on the table next to the bag. She picked up the note and smiled in spite of her annoyance.

Stacy,

Manuel and I decided bravery deserves a reward. He loaned you his comic. (Don't get it dirty!) The doughnuts are for breakfast. (Use the wax paper inside to keep your hands clean.) Try to keep out of trouble for a little while.

See you later.

Kipp

P.S. You never did tell me if you like anchovies on your pizza. Don't worry. Connie will eat them if you don't. Personally, I can't stand them.

Who was Connie? He'd never mentioned her. Feeling vaguely depressed, she decided that Connie must be Kipp and Millie's daughter. Then it dawned on Stacy that her neighbors must have been childhood sweethearts. And their daughter must be quite sophisticated to like anchovies. Stacy began to revise her suspicions. Indeed, Kipp seemed like a family man. Nosy, but still a family man who graciously planned to include her in a safe, informal family dinner.

Removing the lollipop, Stacy looked into the bag and sniffed the aroma of the calorie-laden doughnuts. She chose a particularly gooey chocolate-covered one for starters and set it on her plate, admonishing herself for her weak nature. She placed the container of coffee in the microwave oven and went outside to pick up her daily copy of the *Times*.

A tall, strikingly beautiful, raven-haired woman dressed in a simple lavender pants suit walked toward a late-model sedan parked in the Palmer driveway. She must be Millie, Stacy thought. Millie moved like a fashion model, making her simple outfit look elegant and Stacy feel like a poor churchmouse by comparison. What sane man would cheat on such a stunning woman? Not many. Kipp really was practicing his good neighbor policy. So much for her hasty conclusions!

Millie paused by the car door, glanced up, waved in her direction, and smiled. Not wanting to appear unfriendly, Stacy forced a smile and waved back. In a great pretense of being busy, Stacy scooped up the paper and retreated backward up the path, but not before she noticed a marked resemblance between Kipp and his wife, a fact that wasn't too uncommon. Idly, Stacy wondered which of her two parents Connie favored. Not that it mattered. Both of them were knockouts!

The phone was ringing as she walked in. Rick Samuels's pleasant voice informed her that "Harry" was almost ready. Knowing how eager she was for the blowup he wanted to let her know the delivery was on schedule. Stacy felt relieved. Today was Friday. By this time next week her worries would be over. Now all she needed was to get through tonight.

Then she'd be home free!

She ate two doughnuts, relishing every forbidden morsel! But when she attempted to read the Spanish comic book, she failed miserably. "Reading" the pictures, she ended up supplying her own story.

The day passed quickly. She spent most of it editing a children's story she wanted to submit to *Humpty Dumpty* magazine. By late afternoon she licked the last stamp on the manila envelope and drove to the post office with her manuscript. Praying for an acceptance, she crossed her fingers, handed it to the postal clerk, and headed home.

After glimpsing Millie, Stacy decided she had to make a special effort on her appearance this evening. She chose a simple pink cotton dress with cap

sleeves. The snug bodice dipped low across the
bustline and hugged her rib cage. Shirring accentuated her small waist. The full skirt fell away from the
gentle curve of her hips.

Her makeup brought out the gold flecks in her
hazel eyes, and she applied mascara to the tips of
her lashes. Deciding to wear her hair loose around
her shoulders, she turned away from the mirror
satisfied she'd done her best to make a good first
impression on Millie.

Just as she considered phoning her hostess to
ask when she was expected, her call was delayed by
a sharp rap at the back door. She slipped into san-
dals and went to see who it was.

Kipp, dressed in a navy blue short-sleeved T-shirt
and stark white shorts, leaned against the doorframe
whistling a tune. As soon as he saw Stacy, the tune
became a distinctive wolf whistle. Stacy blushed. If
anyone should be whistling, she should.

Tanned and tall, Kipp was powerfully compelling.
Smiling cornflower-blue eyes crinkled at the corners.
A boyishly wide grin creased his face, accenting the
sexiest cleft Stacy had ever seen this side of a Paul
Newman movie. A medical bag dangled from his left
hand. Balanced on the upturned palm of his right
hand rested a huge pizza box. By her swift calcula-
tions the contents were large enough to feed at least
eight people. And from the nifty mouth-watering
aromas coming from under the lid, she recognized
the ingredients.

She also recognized something else. There was no
wife or child standing next to or behind him!

Craning her neck, Stacy searched past his shoulder, hoping to see his family coming up the walk. He
was alone and obviously expecting to eat at her house,
not his!

She looked up at him quizzically. "Where's Millie and Connie?"

Kipp was nonplussed as he answered her. He seemed to be enjoying the view. "Millie's busy with a previous obligation, but Connie will be along in a minute. You can't push Connie."

That was it? No explanation? Just Millie was busy and Connie couldn't be pushed. She immediately started working up conclusions she could jump to. Only teenagers couldn't be pushed, which confirmed her earlier conclusion that he and Millie married young. After seeing her frumpy neighbor this morning, Millie probably thought it perfectly safe to leave her handsome husband with her teenage daughter while she attended to more important matters.

"Come on, Stacy," Kipp prompted her, a faint smile curving his mouth, "I'm starved. We ought to eat this while it's hot. Enjoying a pizza's a lot like making love, don't you think? The hotter the better."

Stacy's mouth fell open. "I beg your pardon!"

Kipp winked broadly, showing a row of white teeth. He lowered the pizza box and Stacy stepped backward automatically to give him access to the narrow hall. She pressed her spine against the ridge of the cold washing machine. But nature didn't shape Stacy in the form of a board. Her small breasts thrust forward. She couldn't believe he'd try the same trick twice.

But he did. "Oops, sorry. The box is a bit tricky to maneuver." His feeble apology didn't fool her for a second.

The brief contact was over before she could protest. Maybe it was the increased heat from her own body, but Stacy was all too aware of Kipp. Why wasn't the fool wearing long pants? As she trailed him to the kitchen she noticed the muscles in his thighs fairly rippling in delight. No wonder, she thought perversely. In spite of his lousy eating habits, he kept himself in tip-top shape.

It didn't surprise her when Kipp motioned for her to sit down. He already acted as if he owned the place! He ceremoniously placed the box in the center of the table and drew back the lid. Inhaling the contents with a deep breath of gustatory appreciation, he sighed happily.

Stacy watched in fascination as he opened his medical bag. Wiggling his eyebrows, he made a great flourish of fishing something out. When he produced a six-pack of Schlitz, Stacy chuckled. "And here I thought you were a doctor." Kipp was inventive in more ways than one.

He continued setting the table his way. Rules of etiquette didn't faze him. He picked up the napkin container, pulled out a pile of napkins, and dropped a stack in the center of the table. He rummaged through her cupboards to find the plates, then he poked around her utensil drawer for a knife. Spying the doughnut bag at the end of the counter, he made a great show of lifting it up and down as if he were weighing its contents. Withdrawing the two remaining doughnuts, he put them on a plate and brought them to the table.

"How was breakfast?" he asked blandly, crumpling the empty bag.

"Very delicious and very fattening," she admitted sheepishly.

"These are for dessert. And you ate all the chocolate ones. That wasn't fair," he said, a teasing glint in his eye.

"Your note never said I couldn't." She was beginning to relax and enjoy herself. It would be so easy to drown in those compelling blue eyes.

"Are you going out to Kennedy tomorrow?" he asked quietly.

For a moment she looked blank.

"Isn't Harry coming home this weekend?"

"No." She thought fast, dismissing the slightly harsh tone in Kipp's voice. "Harry's in Bombay. Actually he's got the flu. Poor dear, he's laid low."

"How low?"

"Very."

Again an uncomfortably clear vision of her nose growing like Pinocchio's flashed through her mind. She picked up a beer, feigning great interest in the can.

"That's a new one on me," Kipp said, obviously deep in thought.

"What is?"

"The Bombay flu. Didn't you tell me yesterday he was in England? I've heard of the Hong Kong and the Russian flu, but never the Bombay flu. So when is he coming home?"

His questions and her lies were unnerving her. She tilted her beer and sipped it. Kipp finished his can of beer, opened another, and sat sipping while his eyes never left her face.

"You never told me what Harry does."

"If I told you he works undercover, would you believe me?"

"Actually, I think I would. His type of traveling is consistent with cloak-and-dagger work. So that's why you've been hemming and hawing. How undercover?" he asked boldly.

"Very. Now, please forget I told you, or I could get in trouble. I've never been so careless before." She gulped, averting his eyes. "Shouldn't Connie be coming in?" It was time she met her teenage chaperone.

Kipp took a long sip of beer before answering. "There's no rush. Connie'll be in soon."

"How old is Connie?" Stacy reached for a slice of the oozing pizza. She fervently hoped Connie would jump on her father if he stepped out of line.

"I can't be too sure. Pretty young. I'm not too good on birthdays," he said, surprising her so much she nearly dropped her pizza.

"Young young?" she queried, and when he nodded, she exploded. "How could you leave Connie alone?" she demanded. "Anything could happen."

Rubbing his hands together with relish, Kipp lifted the lid of the box, setting her temper up another notch. She'd expected him to bring his daughter in now at least. Instead, he took another appreciative sniff of the box's contents.

"Nothing's going to happen," he said offhandedly. "The gate's closed. Ah-ha, smell that. I guarantee you, one whiff and Connie will beat it in here. I hope you left the back door open."

"I most certainly did not!" she replied huffily.

She could have been throwing a temper tantrum for all the attention he paid to her outburst. His low chuckle followed her on her indignant march to the back door. She was fuming at herself for being attracted to him, a married man whose parenting left much to be desired! How could she allow this wretch in her house . . . in her life?

She heard the scratching sound just as she reached the door. What was with this crazy family? Kipp was in there laughing at his own secret joke, Millie had taken a powder, leaving a young child in the custody of a father who didn't know her exact age and to top it off, the poor little thing scratched on doors like an animal. No wonder teaching was hard. The parents were nuts!

As she opened the door, a blur of brown fur moving at great speed streaked past her and she yelped in surprise. "Watch it," she called to Kipp, "there's a horse loose in here!"

"I wouldn't let Connie hear you say that if I were you," Kipp shouted. "He's mixed up enough, thinking he's human. Now, come on in, Mrs. Jump-to-Conclusions Conklin, and let's eat."

Stacy loosened her death grip on the doorknob. She felt the hair on the back of her neck stand at attention. He'd tricked her.

With murder in her eyes Stacy reentered the room, wishing she were tall enough to wipe the smug grin off Kipp's face. His eyes danced merrily. The corners of his mouth curved upward in pure mischief, a tall version of Peck's Bad Boy.

"Sorry about the little joke, but you should have seen your face. You were so certain I'd leave a child alone, I couldn't resist letting you meet Connie for yourself. Now can you see why I wasn't sure of my child's birthday? And by the way," he said pointedly, "he's my son, not my daughter. You're welcome to check for yourself."

"I'll take your word for it," she murmured weakly, praying the color of her face blended well with pink. Trying to salvage her pride, she asked, "Isn't Connie a girl's name?"

He leaned down to drop anchovies on Connie's plate. "Connie's named for Conrad Hilton. I found this pooch wandering the hallways when I stayed at the Los Angeles Hilton. How that animal ever got past the lobby, I'll never know." She watched as Connie greedily gulped down some anchovies.

"If you keep feeding him those, you won't have him long."

"Anchovies are mild," Kipp said, dismissing her

concern. "This character is weird. His favorite foods are brussels sprouts and sushi." As if on cue, Connie favored them with a gratifying belch. Kipp's lip curled in disgust.

"He's a two-time flunkee from obedience school. I've tried everything. Ed says it's best to leave him alone. If we push him too much, we fracture his personality."

"Who's Ed?" she asked weakly.

"His psychiatrist."

Stacy collapsed in the nearest chair and laughed at Kipp's nonsense. "Do you actually mean you took this puppy to a shrink?"

"Wouldn't you? He's bizarre."

"What did Ed say?" she asked, wondering who was bizarre, Kipp or the dog.

"About what you'd expect. Ed said he wouldn't charge me anything for Connie, but he'd give me professional courtesy for treatment."

Kipp reminded her of a kid testing the gullibility of his parents. She couldn't be sure if his wild tale was true.

Above the panting animal, summer-blue eyes captured sparkling hazel ones. Stacy's gaze drifted to the linoleum floor as she pretended great interest in the geometric pattern. When she dared to look again at Kipp, she found he was still watching her. Drawn by his steady glance, Stacy shivered. Her heart thrummed crazily. She'd seen that heated look on his face in her dreams just before he'd pulled her into his arms and buried his head at her breasts. There was something sensuous and sinfully alluring as his hooded eyes assessed her silently. She felt the color in her cheeks and knew he saw it too.

Kipp shifted in his seat, then lifted the can of beer to his mouth. A bit of white foam stuck to his lips and he slowly licked it away. She imagined those lips where they'd been in her dream and wondered again if he'd seen her naked. She opened her mouth in a silent plea for him to stop his blatant perusal. His eyes momentarily flicked to her lips, then downward to her chest. Her nipples tingled with awareness, straining for his touch.

Knowing that he knew what he was doing and knowing he knew that she knew made the game he was playing with her all the more dangerous. It took all her control to keep from shouting for him to stop.

"You were in my room again last night. Was I—?" She couldn't believe she'd actually asked him.

"You were." He answered the question that had been plaguing her all day. Flustered, she reached for her beer, knocking it over. Kipp stood up, grabbing the pile of napkins. But when he removed the can from her shaking fingers, the heat from his hand burned a fiery path up her arms.

"Stacy," he said quietly, "I see bodies all the time."

"Oh, my," she confessed on an audible sigh, "when I think of what was going through my mind."

"I know what was going through your mind."

Not everything, she thought thankfully. At least he'd never know how he had kissed her in her dream.

She calmed down as he continued to mop up the spilled liquid. When he was through, he gave her a clean plate.

"Friends?" he asked, serving a slice of pizza to her.

"Friends," she answered, yet wondered how that could be.

Stacy took a bite of pizza. Cheeze oozed over the sides of the slice and her tongue flicked at the crusty underside, taking the warm topping between her teeth. She glanced up. Kipp hadn't touched the food on his plate.

"The pizza's delicious," she said. "It's too bad Millie's missing it."

Kipp wanted to throttle the teasing wench. She knew damn well what she was doing to him. Her and her educated tongue!

Never taking his eyes from her he brought his slice of pizza to his lips. He suffered in silent misery when he bit the tender flesh inside his cheek. Stacy was killing him!

Uttering an oath, he dropped the piece on his plate and took a healthy swig of beer. Mesmerized, he continued to observe Stacy as her tongue flicked out to catch the stringy cheese. Didn't the little vixen have the faintest idea of the havoc she was wreaking? He couldn't stand up if he wanted to. Hell, she was no innocent. Dragging on his beer for comfort, he thought about women and the tricks they played on poor, unsuspecting men. Wasn't that why he never told her he was divorced? His blood boiling, he tore open another can of beer and put it to his lips. Three empty cans lined up in front of him like so many soldiers. Damn. He couldn't eat while she sat there devouring her pizza like that.

"Did you have a dog when you were a little boy?" Stacy asked before puckering her lips and nibbling at a long string of cheese.

When he could breathe again, he answered her curtly. "No."

"That explains it," she said blithely, ignoring his testy manner. "Little boys often feed their dogs forbidden foods. All it means is that you love your pet. And, of course, you're reverting to a second childhood."

"Not in everything," he said in flat disagreement.

Second childhood, his foot! No child experienced this kind of sweet torture. His eyes grew stormy. She was wearing it again tonight, a provocative scent of jasmine which the odor of the beer didn't block. That perfume had driven him crazy the night before, when he had carried her up the stairs. She was driving him crazy now, and all she could talk about was his damned dog.

He hated Connie now. He hated the way he nuzzled his big fat head on her lap and gazed at her with his moon eyes. He hated seeing her stroke Connie's head. He hated Stacy for what she was doing to him and he hated himself for reacting the way he was. But he knew he didn't really hate her or Connie, so he was back where he started from—nowhere!

"Why aren't you eating? I thought you said you were starved."

Damn her for acting so prissily concerned, Kipp thought, but he said, "I want to relax a little while first." His voice sounded odd. He shrugged his broad shoulders and adjusted himself painfully in the chair.

She looked blissfully content, licking and eating with one hand and massaging Connie's head with the other.

He grew more uncomfortable.

What would she say, he wondered, if she knew how much he wanted her? What would Hippocrates say? He was hungry, but not for food. He resented Stacy's chasing away his normally huge appetite. Now he didn't know which was worse: watching her eat or watching her not eat. Still, his eyes stayed glued to the object of his misery. She was a brazen hussy who apparently delighted in disrobing in plain sight of his telescope. She even made a mockery of his hobby!

None of what he was feeling was his fault, he reasoned sensibly as the beer slid down his throat. He was, after all, a mere mortal. Suppose, just suppose he told her he wasn't married? What good would it do? She was.

"What do you do?" There was an edge to his voice and she glanced at him quizzically. She patted her lips with her napkin and placed it near her plate.

"Do?" She licked a dainty finger and he moaned inwardly.

"Yes, do? As in when you're not playing in the dirt."

"Oh, that. I teach third grade and I write on the side."

"What do you write?"

"Children's stuff mostly." It wasn't necessary to add that Harry scoffed at her attempts. He thought she should be writing adult books where, he claimed, the money was. "Why aren't you eating? There's enough here for an army."

"That explains it."

"What?" She was having trouble following his abrupt change in subjects.

"The feeling that I have to be on my best behavior. You know, I was in love with my third grade teacher. It nearly broke my heart. I was eight and she was twenty-eight and married. I remember she was fun-loving. Are you fun-loving, Stacy?" he asked softly, watching the expression on her face change.

The silly banter ceased. Good, he thought, that got her attention away from the damned pizza. His head was beginning to spin and it was her fault. His whole body desired her and that was her fault too.

"Kipp," he heard her say, "I have to get an early start in the morning. I imagine you do too. Maybe we should call it a night?" She stood up without waiting for his reply.

Kipp stared at her for a moment. Then he nodded in agreement. The chair made a scuffing sound in back of him. He cleared the table, washed his hands, and picked up his medical bag. "Let me check your hands. This time I'll put a respectable-sized bandage on. I swathed them with extra gauze only to make sure you stayed out of trouble."

"Do you think you should?" she asked, sounding full of doubt.

"I'm not drunk," he said gruffly, and he knew he wasn't. He almost wished he were, but he wasn't.

Stacy waited, quietly conscious of his hands on her, his body heat wreaking havoc with her own breathing. He removed the old bandages, cleaned and dressed the wounds, and applied neat small gauze pads. He touched only her hands yet she felt branded all over. She'd seen the longing in his eyes and hoped he couldn't read hers.

"There, that about fixes them. Keep them clean. I'll leave some salve and Band-Aids for you. Repeat the process for the next day or so, then let the air get at them."

So he wasn't coming back. Good, she thought. It was better.

From the corner of the room Connie's long body shivered in energetic anticipation. Suddenly, without warning, he reared upright and lunged playfully.

Startled, Stacy pitched forward. "Oh," she cried. The small space between her body and Kipp's evaporated. Her arms reached up and her hands clasped the base of Kipp's neck. Her fingers delved into his hair. She felt his arms swoop around her waist, holding her so tightly their bodies strained intimately against each other's. Feminine softness met male hardness, womanly curves to male arousal. Thigh pressed against thigh, and her full breasts flattened against a firm, muscular chest.

Her dream took on a life of its own.

Instinct told her he was going to kiss her. *Move!* a warning voice screamed in her head. She felt his quickened breath mingle with her own; she read the indecision in his eyes.

He read the panic in hers. His arms stroked her back, gentling her like a baby. His lips hovered over hers.

She was the nectar.

He was the bee.

Just before his mouth swooped over hers she heard him mutter, "Forgive me. I can't help myself."

And neither could she. Fear and caution fled as her subconscious and conscious desires met and mingled. As in her dream, she reached hungrily for him. His lips rocked across her mouth, setting off shock wave after shock wave. Their mouths fused and she felt him play with her bottom lip, stroking, stroking back and forth. She sought his tongue and bit it in passion. His mouth opened hot and demanding. She accepted greedily. Her lips parted, giving him ready access. Warm and firm, he drank with an unquenchable thirst. Their tongues played a ritual mating game where they were both losers and winners.

Her control slipped away. His eager kiss unleashed an avalanche of suppressed emotions and his hands, as they cupped her buttocks, straining her closer, evoked long-unfelt desires in her. They fit together like pieces of a jigsaw puzzle. One hand moved to hold her head captive. The other inched between them to stroke her breast. He played with the hard nub of her nipple. She felt as if every nerve in her body were centered at whatever place his fingers touched her. She felt how much he desired her as he rotated his hips. Suddenly she was shocked back into reality. The kitchen came into focus. She heard Connie whining for attention, the clock ticking on the wall.

Was it she who first broke the kiss? Gulping for breath, they pulled away from each other by degrees, listening to the tattoo of the other's heartbeat.

For Kipp the kiss was everything he was afraid it would be.

For Stacy the kiss was forbidden fruit.

Wordlessly they stared. Stacy tried to speak, but no words came. Their stunned expressions reflected the knowledge that theirs was no idle kiss. It had shattered both of them, leaving them shaking with desire. Cursing the fates, Kipp leaned his forehead against Stacy's.

He placed his fingers on her lips. In a voice striving for control, he whispered hoarsely, "Don't say anything. Only listen. None of this was your fault. It was mine. Maybe it was all the beer, maybe it was Connie pushing you into my arms, I don't know. All I know is that I promise it won't happen again. You don't have to be afraid."

He stepped back, tilting her chin up, his worried eyes searching her passion-drugged eyes. Unwittingly, he said the one thing calculated to make her feel cheap.

"Harry need never know."

Stacy bit her rising hysteria. Stammering, she played out her role in the farce. "Millie?" How was she going to face his wife?

"Believe me"—Kipp's eyes drilled into hers—"I have no intention of telling her."

Kipp gathered up his medical bag. Connie quietly

padded after his master. The door closed softly behind Kipp.

The full force of Kipp's suggestion made Stacy feel guiltier than ever. Tears stung her eyes. Her hands clenched in tight balls by her sides. She'd behaved like a shameless hussy. He'd been drinking and that was a feeble excuse. What excuse did she have?

In the future she'd be more careful. Next week "Harry" would protect her from herself and Kipp. What a joke, she thought ruefully. Harry had never made her feel the way Kipp did.

School would begin next week. Then her life would revert to an orderly routine and she could forget the man next door who belonged to another woman.

Five

Hope, Stacy soon learned, might spring eternal, but in her case it had sprung a constant leak. Each time she tried to bail Kipp out of her thoughts, he bobbed to the surface again.

She missed him.

The plain, simple, indisputably dangerous fact was she missed him.

In the two weeks since her "fall from grace," as she came to think of it, she studiously avoided him by remaining behind locked doors until he left for his morning jog. By now she knew he was a creature of habit, backhanding the morning paper onto his front porch before taking off in a fast run. Once he'd turned the corner and the coast was clear she'd zoom her car out of the garage and head for work.

School should have been the one place for her to wipe Kipp out of her mind. Heaven knew, she was busy enough. But even there he'd turn up at the most unpredictable times.

Stacy made a practice of ending each day for her students with a story created just for them. She illustrated her tales as she spoke with bold strokes of crayon on a large artist's pad. Usually her students were spellbound by the stories.

One day her hand swept across the pad controlled by an invisible force more powerful than conscious thought. For the first time, her sketching commanded the characters and the developing story line rather than the other way around. Soon there appeared on the pad a giraffe examining a patient. He wore his doctor's bag around his long neck. To the children's delight and her absolute horror, the giraffe had blue eyes and a thatch of thick brown hair. Hanging on the wall in back of him, his medical diploma declared him to be Dr. Jerome Giraffe. Looking trustingly into his eyes—his twinkling blue eyes—was Manuela Marsupial, a little kangaroo clutching a Spanish-language comic book. So startled was Stacy by the "ghost drawing" that she half-expected Kipp to walk into her classroom door and introduce himself as the real Dr. Jerome Giraffe.

That's when she knew she was in as deep a mess of trouble in the daytime as she was at night!

Technically, there wasn't any reason for her not to be able to sleep through the night undisturbed. Practically, as long as the real-life Kipp slumbered in a bed across the way from hers, it was impossible. Especially when she knew Millie had first dibs on his body while the only thing she had first dibs on was a blue-eyed giraffe!

Try as she might to erase the little characters from her mind, they'd creep back in again and demand attention. Finally, she decided to do the only thing she could to exorcise Kipp. She would put him and his animal form down on paper, write his story, and mail him out of her life right to the nearest publisher! Day after day she'd come home from

school, eat a hurried meal, and dash to her typewriter, where she'd write until she was bleary-eyed,
dropping like a wrung-out dishrag into bed. Then
she'd wait for the bliss of sleep.

A fat lot of good it did!

Kipp managed to intrude everywhere. She dreamed
about him. Sometimes he starred as one of the heroes from her favorite book or movie. More often
than not he starred in repeat performances, swag-
gering in devil-may-care fashion across her brain.
Disgusted with her unfulfilled dreams, she thought
if she saw him once more dressed as Rhett Butler,
or herself as Scarlett, she'd wake up with a full-
fledged southern accent!

Which was why she allowed Bev to talk her into
her first date. "Now you're cooking," Bev said in
ecstatic approval.

Stacy cringed at the idea, but she had to do something drastic before the bags under her eyes needed packing or she became a sleeping-pill junkie!
One way or the other she was determined to drive
Kipp out of her mind.

"What's involved?" Stacy asked Bev.

"What do you mean involved? Nothing's involved.
I swear, you're the most finicky person I know. Do
you realize other women would kill to meet an eligi-
ble doctor? It's every divorcée's dream. All you have
to do is show up. Naturally, I expect you to look
smashing. Buy something new and sexy and wear
those Christian Dior patterned stockings. Black. No
other color. You've got great legs. Might as well show
them off."

"I think I'm getting sick." Stacy picked up a hand
mirror from the night table near her bed. Sticking
out her tongue, she took one look in the mirror at
her bloodshot eyes. Just the thought of getting back

into the dating world caused her head to pound. Then she glanced at "Harry's" smiling puss and her resolve strengthened.

"Stop being so scared, Stacy. The odds are in your favor. You have nothing to lose."

"Does Vito mind?" she asked anxiously.

"Leave that to me. If you like what you see, take it from there. We'll make up a signal. If you think he's got possibilities, do what Lauren Bacall did. Whistle."

Not in a million years! she thought after she hung up. Rummaging in her drawer for a newly bought package of darts, she aimed the rubber-tipped missile at "Harry," hitting him straight on the nose.

"Harry, you rat, it's all your fault! I do not need to fall for a married man! I do not need this complication in my life! Furthermore, I caught hell in a meeting today for not paying attention. Not that the principal was saying anything earth-shattering, mind you, but I do need my job. Which"—she squinted and snapped out another dart—"is more important to me than ever, thanks to you!"

"Harry's" shiny face began to resemble a pin cushion. Realizing with dismay she was on the road to ruining her photographic line of defense, she bounced out of bed and draped "Harry's" head with a paper bag. On the weekends she'd been dragging the cumbersome figure from the opposite wall to his post to stand guard duty behind the partially opened curtains.

Stacy purposely disregarded Bev's advice as she dressed for Saturday night. She was not interested in vamping a man she'd never met. If Vito's new associate preferred the hot-tomato type, he'd be none the sadder when she told him her husband was out of town. Opting for the aloof sophisticated look, she chose a beige cashmere sheath and textured beige stockings. She styled her blonde tresses in a French plait.

She might look the picture of cool, she thought, but her insides felt as if she were about to go over Niagara Falls in a barrel. Vaguely wondering if other divorced women went through these nervous, clutchy feelings, she thought about Kipp. Why were all the good ones married? Kipp was honorable though. He'd made a mistake, true, but he'd kept his word and hadn't tried to see her again.

As she dabbed perfume behind her ears and on her wrists, she gave a last critical glance at herself in the mirror and hastily applied more blush to accentuate her high cheekbones and her wide-set eyes.

To guard against the early fall chill, she tossed a teal blue wool cape in the backseat of her Datsun. But when she turned the key in the ignition, nothing happened.

"Damn you, battery, why did you pick this moment to drop dead?" she wailed inside the empty garage.

Through her rearview mirror she noticed Kipp pulling out of his driveway. She knew if she honked her horn he'd stop and jump-start the battery. And then what? Create an embarrassing situation?

Tapping her hands on the steering wheel, she refused to call it quits now that she'd dressed and psyched herself up. Determined to see the evening through no matter what, she returned to the kitchen and phoned for a cab to drive her to her friend's sprawling ranch home.

•　　•　　•

"Don't tell me after all this he's a no-show?" Stacy asked as she followed Bev into the spacious knotty pine-paneled den.

"Not at all. Vito called. They'll be here soon."

"And—?"

"And judge for yourself. I met him briefly when I brought Jeff to Vito's office for his booster shots. Naturally I assumed he was married. He'd popped in to examine some X rays. Jeff took to him immediately. Knowing my son, that has to mean something. I don't know his story, but I sure wouldn't pass up an opportunity to find out. If you do, you're crazy. My Italian vibes don't lie. He's tall and terrific."

"What's his name?"

"Oh, no. No questions. I know you. You'll try to wheedle everything out of me, decide he's not for you, and leave before he walks in the door."

Stacy laughed. Bev knew her too well. "You're sure he doesn't have an inkling as to my real reason for being here?"

"He doesn't even know you'll be here. You're too much of a worrywart. What could happen?" Bev patted her arm.

"What did you tell Vito?" A guarded note crept into Stacy's voice.

"You drive me crazy. I told Vito that if he ever wants to warm his hands on my backside again not to say anything about you. You, my dear, are going to be a complete surprise. Like a nude coming out of a cake. Satisfied?"

In spite of herself, Stacy felt a bubble of excitement. She was also a nervous wreck. Her palms were damp. One minute she was sorry she agreed to Bev's scheme, the next minute she wanted to view the man through a one-way mirror. Then the next minute she was filled with a wild desire to run.

Instead, she rose and went into the bathroom for a last-minute check on her appearance. Except for the wary brightness in her eyes, a stranger wouldn't know the blond woman in the designer clothes wasn't as cool as a cucumber. Only she knew that she felt like throwing up.

Almost immediately she recognized Vito's booming hello. She gripped the marble bowl tightly. Her fingers were white. Stacy counted to ten and took a deep breath. Head high, she opened the door. Consciously placing one foot in front of the other, she felt as if she were walking the plank.

From the den came the sound of glasses clinking in a toast. She heard a deep masculine voice say "Prost." Soon this was followed by the joined laughter of Bev and Vito. In the hall, out of sight, Stacy paused for a moment to gather her courage.

"Ah, here she is." Vito's friendly wave propelled her toward the gathering. Stacy glided into the room, a smile spread lightly over her features.

"Stacy Conklin, I'd like you to meet Kipp Palmer."

Kipp! The sight of him knocked the wind out of her. She froze in her tracks. She didn't even recognize the cry from her lips.

"You!"

Kipp's eyes widened imperceptibly. His dimpled grin clearly showed delight at the surprise.

Putting his glass on the bar, he stepped forward and wrapped her small hand firmly in his. His eyes traveled the length of her dress, noting the perfect roundness of her breasts, the sensuous curve of her hips, her flat tummy and slim waist. Her hair sleekly drawn back from her face perfectly framed its oval shape and brought into stunning relief the huge eyes staring at him in shock.

"Well, well, well," he said, gazing down at her. "It seems we're fortunate enough to know the same people. You're looking especially lovely tonight, Stacy. I must say clothes suit you. This is the first time I've seen you fully dressed, isn't it?"

A strangled sound escaped her throat. She snatched her hand from his. She wasn't about to remind him that when he kissed her she was wearing a pink dress.

"Excuse me, do you two know each other?" Bev asked.

"Obviously," Stacy snapped, whipping her head toward her startled friend. "How could you?"

"What?" Bev's glass dripped moisture on the parquet floor, but she didn't notice.

"Invite this impostor!"

"Now, just a minute," Kipp protested. "I'm no impostor."

"No?" Stacy exclaimed, her hands on her hips. "Where's Millie?"

"Millie's with Frank."

"A convenient story. The last time she was at a meeting or something. You never did say."

"For Pete's sake, who's Frank?" Vito asked. "Will one of you please enlighten me?"

Both ignored their host and hostess, who stared at them in confusion.

"Who's Millie?" Bev interjected. "Vito, do you know what's going on here?"

Vito cocked his head at their guests. "I haven't got the faintest idea. You ask them."

"Kipp, why don't *you* tell us who Millie and Frank really are? It seems the only identity I can vouch for is Connie's."

"Who's Connie?" Bev and Vito timed their question perfectly, and it came out in unison.

"Where's Harry?" Kipp bellowed, turning the attack on Stacy, his face suffused with irritation.

"Home," Stacy lied bravely, and Kipp's thick brows shot up.

"Home?" Bev and Vito shouted at the same time.

Kipp's belligerent eyes focused on his opponent. "Why isn't your hubby here? Don't tell me he's tired of glaring out the window every weekend. What did you tell him about us?"

"Nothing," Stacy retorted sarcastically. "I don't owe you any explanations." She jabbed a pink fingernail on the vest of Kipp's three-piece blue pinstriped suit. He didn't have to look like an ad for *Gentlemen's Quarterly*. Why couldn't he just look like the bum he was?

Bev bounced on her toes, vying for attention. "Well, I'd appreciate an explanation. This is better than *General Hospital*. Stop pinching me, Vito. She's my friend."

"Bev, stop cannon-loading," Stacy said stiffly. "I'm going. You people go on with your dinner."

"Like hell you're going. You and I are going to talk," Kipp interjected.

Kipp moved with the quickness of a sprinter. He grabbed Stacy's wrist, half-pulling, half-dragging the protesting bundle of female fury out the front door. Over his shoulder he called an apology to a gaping Bev and Vito.

"Excuse us. We'll be right back."

The night air was chilly, not a night to be without a wrap. But neither noticed the temperature. Releasing Stacy's wrist, Kipp blocked her escape by sandwiching her between him and the outside brick wall of the house. On either side of her neck a long, jacketed arm trapped her as effectively as if she were a caged animal.

Stacy hurled her invectives at him, forgetting her own duplicity. "What an impostor you are! Bev said she invited a friend of Vito's."

"She did. We work together."

Stacy didn't buy his nonchalant explanation. "A *divorced* friend. Don't you think that's a little underhanded, to say the least? I knew you didn't have a sterling character, but palming yourself off as a divorced man is too much."

"Why? It's the truth."

"Aren't you overlooking Millie? You said . . .?"

Clearly exasperated, he added more fuel to the fire. "I *said*, if you care to think back, I *said* Millie wanted to bake me a cake. I *said* she couldn't join us for pizza. I *said* she had another obligation. I *never* said she was my wife. That was your idea, not mine, Mrs. Jump-to-Conclusions Conklin."

"Who's Millie?"

"My twin sister. Frank's her husband."

"Twin!" Stacy marveled at the glibness of Kipp's tongue. Then she felt the first stirrings of doubt. She digested the news as she teetered slightly on her heels. Kipp's arms moved to steady her, but she swiftly pushed them out of the way.

"And what about your noble little speech?"

"What noble speech?"

"The one," she said, her eyes spitting fire, "where you promised never to tell Millie about our . . . Oh, nuts!"

His mouth quirked, suppressing the word she refused to utter.

"That was easy for you to do," she went on. "What brother tells his own sister he tried to put the make on a married woman? Hah! And how magnanimously you suggested Harry need never know. Of course not, you two-timing bum! You didn't want to get bopped in the head by an irate husband. Ooh, when I think of the sucker you played me for when all the time you were kissing—"

With one lithe movement he grabbed her upper arms. "Now, listen to me, you little fool. That was quite a sweeping indictment of my character. Granted, I didn't clear up the misconception about Millie. I'm sorry about that, but I had my reasons. I'm not sorry about kissing you. It's all I've thought about since it happened. I've wanted to break down your door and do it again."

"You're a fine one to talk! Why did you let me believe you were married?" Her angry breath warmed his cheeks and he swore softly.

There was a heavy pause as Kipp contemplated her question. One way or the other, her opinion of him couldn't get much lower. His eyes made a thorough study of her face, from her flushed cheeks to the pinpoints of light dancing in her eyes. His jaw tensed.

"You know and I know that if you thought you were sharing a pizza with a bachelor, you'd have said no in the first place. Especially since I'd been in your house in the middle of the night and seen you half naked. Right?"

"You're damn right," she said tartly, glaring at him. He returned her penetrating stare as her mind raced with his revelation.

"How long were you planning on keeping up the game of Let's Pretend?" she asked silkily. When he didn't immediately answer, she snapped, "Cat got your tongue?"

A study in tight control, he towered over her. "Until I was good and ready, and you can stow the rancor, Stacy. I've had enough of that to last a lifetime."

Spurred on by a hollow sense of rejection she didn't take the time to examine, she disregarded his warning. "Of course, our living in such close proximity made things a bit hairy, didn't they? On the other hand, in my deluded state I did provide some entertainment for you!"

"Don't say anything you'll be sorry for. That isn't true and you know it!"

Overlooking her own mendacity, she spit out the rest. "Oh, but you're wrong. We're not out here because you had an urge for honesty. Am I right?" Her bright eyes widened for a moment. Then her lashes flickered downward and she seemed to withdraw to some inner place.

Even as she was flinging her barbs at him she was shocked at her waspish tone. After all, this was a simple case of tit-for-tat, sauce for the goose sauce for the gander. So why was she so furious? How could she cast the first stone? She was no better than he in the truth department!

Kipp tensed visibly. Then, studying the subtle changes in her flushed face, he probed, "Is there another reason my marital status is so important to you?" His eyes impaled hers, willing her to be honest.

"I don't like being made a fool of," she mumbled, more upset with the varied emotions bombarding her heart than she cared to admit.

"I never meant to make a fool of you," he replied gently, reaching out to touch her cheek. Confused and embarrassed, she turned her head away from his questing eyes.

Releasing a deep breath, he jammed his hands into his pockets. "Maybe it's time I explained why I kept up the pretense." He took her silence as permission to continue.

"My marriage was a terrible mistake. When you

and I first met, I was still putting the pieces of my life back together. Ever since my divorce, people have been trying to fix me up with dates. And by the way, what you said before was true." She glanced up quickly. Looking deeply into her eyes, he said, "I do like to do my own choosing. Anyway, I wanted to get off by myself to sort things out. That's the reason I rented the house for a year." He paused and she felt his breath feathering her hair.

"A divorce is devastating. You feel as if you're missing an appendage. For a while you go around like an emotional cripple in a world of healthy people. Work becomes your salvation. You function, you smile, you talk, but all the while inside, where nobody can see, you're dying by stages, a little at a time. It took me quite a while to sort out the guilt and the anger. In the end I decided to stop wearing a hair shirt and live."

Stacy bit back the lump rising in her throat. She'd felt guilty, too, blaming herself for every argument, spinning them over in her mind like a top gone haywire. It was only recently, after much soul-searching, that she realized Harry's impulsiveness stemmed from the powerful forces that shaped his childhood. His mother had died long before she met him. He'd told her that his father gambled heavily. A frequent visitor to Las Vegas, he simply failed to come home after one of his trips. Harry had been ten years old.

The details of Harry's adolescence were sketchy. Stacy had been too blindly infatuated with the tall, handsome heartthrob to look beyond the surface. After they married, she'd grown up fast, assuming the responsible role of wife and wage earner. As the years passed, she was saddened and disappointed that he flitted from job to job. With the wisdom of hindsight she realized his life-of-the-party veneer hid deep feelings of insecurity. Where once there'd been love in her heart, now there was only a feeling of emptiness.

Listening to Kipp share his feelings was like hearing a recital of her own. He'd described all the stages she'd gone through. Hot tears welled up in her eyes. Blinking rapidly, she wiped the dampness away with the back of her hand before Kipp could see it. She confronted the hard truth. They were kindred spirits. More than that. He'd become important to her and she had needlessly fought to banish him.

"And now, Kipp, are you back in circulation?"

"Hardly," he said. "I bitterly regret choosing the wrong partner in the first place. Felicia and I were as unsuited to each other as two people can be. Her image of being a doctor's wife was to attend a constant round of social benefits and getting her picture in the society columns. When she found out my late nights and long hours interfered with her fairy-tale image, things got ugly.

"We didn't see eye to eye on the important things like having children. She didn't want to ruin her figure. It wasn't until after the marriage ceremony that I learned that tidbit of information. She was beautiful only on the outside. I guess I didn't help. Maybe if I spent more time with her, she wouldn't have felt the need to resort to subterfuge."

"Subterfuge?"

"*Affairs* is a better word," he snorted, penciling his fingers through his thick brown mane. "I came home early one day." His voice took on a hard edge. "It was quite an eye-opener to find my wife in a compromising situation. You have no idea how many times since then I wished I'd stayed at the office. We even tried to talk over our problems. Neither of us was ready to stop blaming the other. Felicia hid behind lies. Pretty soon the lies built on more lies."

Stacy flinched as his mouth tightened ominously.

"Our marriage was like a swaying ladder. It was bound to topple. There was no place for it to go but down. We both recognized the end. So finally we called a halt to the sham. Do you know that during our divorce we were actually nicer to each other than during our marriage?"

Filled with an inexplicable surge of resentment and jealousy, Stacy asked quietly, "Are you still in love with her?"

"In love with her?" he answered, and she felt the angry reaction of his fingers biting into her upper arms. "Hell, no. It's more disgust with myself for acting like some damned kid who couldn't wait to jump in the sack. All those wasted years with nothing to show for it."

How many nights had she lain awake thinking similar thoughts? How many nights had she hidden behind her typewriter, seeking the release given by her lively imagination?

Choices. All of life comes down to choices. If you're lucky, you make the right ones. If not, you become a statistic with all the lonely nights on the calendar to prove it.

How explicitly he put her own personal demons into words! The anger washed out of her, leaving her feeling drained. Tears stung the lids of her eyes. She wanted to lay her head against the broad solid wall of his chest. She wanted to croon to him to erase the hurt in his eyes. She wanted to reach up and soothe away the tightly controlled line of his lips, to bring his mouth down to hers. Surely, if she understood his pain, he'd understand hers.

Cautious by nature and aware that their hosts

were wondering why they were taking so long to settle their differences, Stacy kept from blurting out the truth. It was as if a great sense of peace invaded her system. Before the evening ended she would tell Kipp about Harry, but she would do it at home, where she would be free from pressure.

"Hey," he said gruffly, cupping her chin in his large hand and forcing her to look at him, "I didn't mean to unload on you. What is there about you that loosens my tongue? Ever since we met I've had the strangest feeling you'd understand. And there's another thing you should know as long as I'm coming clean. When I held you in my arms and we kissed, it felt right and good. And heaven help me, I want to kiss you right now."

There was no question, no conscious decision on her part. It was as natural as breathing for her to melt into his arms. His hands went around her waist. Hers went around his neck. She wrapped her fingers in the thickness of his hair. As he bent his head, erasing the distance between them, she closed her eyes. When his lips touched hers it was as though he were seeking and she were giving comfort in the most elemental way a woman could give to a man. With her lips fused to his she breathed in his over-powering male scent. She knew a sweeter pain than she ever thought possible.

She heard him murmur, "Sweet, oh, Lord, you're so sweet."

His hands slid up and down the sides of her body. Then, as if she weren't close enough, they moved down her spine, pressing her closer still. He kissed her eyes and her cheeks. When his lips trailed a fiery path along her jaw, she arched her neck.

In some remote corner of her mind Stacy knew she should stop him. They were standing outside in the cold, but all she could feel was the burning heat from his body, his slightly rough beard on her cheek, his hands trailing a knowing path. She buried all practical thoughts, banished everything but the sensations that were turning her insides to jelly.

Thrusting all shame to the side, Stacy met the increasing urgency of his kiss. His tongue was given ready access to the soft interior of her mouth. Moaning, she leaned into him and clung to him with a rush of joy.

Her eager response sped through him like a brush fire gone wild. All his male experience told him she wasn't promiscuous, couldn't be kissing him this way unless she, too, felt the rightness of their being together. It had happened every time. At first he had wondered why. Now he didn't give a damn. Only their union could douse the hot flames consuming him.

He kissed her greedily and moved his hand up to cup her breast. His fingers kneaded the nipple aroused by his touch. The last remnant of his self-control vanished as he bent his head down to taste what his fingers had known.

With a distinct effort Stacy pushed her hands between them, creating a small space. It was all happening too fast. The timing was all wrong. "Kipp . . . please. We can't. Bev is probably wondering why we're out here so long."

His passion-dazed eyes pinpointed his desire. "Stacy, we can't leave it this way. Not this time. It isn't over between us. You know that, don't you?"

"Yes," she whispered, wishing they were already home. "I'll drive home with you. My car's on the fritz and I came by cab. We have to talk."

"I agree," he answered positively, "but we're not going to talk in the car. We're going to my house."

She knew he'd said that because he thought Harry was home in bed. With a start she realized "Harry" was still in the window. She'd forgotten to hide him for the night! No matter. She had one last act of legerdemain to perform. When they arrived home, she'd make up an excuse, run upstairs and remove "Harry" before going over to Kipp's house. After listening to his angry account of Felicia's schemes, the last thing she needed was to have him discover the lengths of her own imaginative plot!

Six

"Okay. What gives with you two? You guys were out there so long I almost sent out the troops." Bev corralled Stacy and dragged her into the kitchen on the pretense of needing help with serving dinner. Sitting down on a kitchen chair, she announced, "We're not moving until you tell me the whole story. And don't say there's nothing to tell or I'll kill you. I know you, kiddo, the high color in your cheeks and that starry-eyed gaze in your eyes didn't come from the weather. So shoot!"

"Well . . ." Stacy began slowly, deliberately teasing. Bev shot her a menaeing look and Stacy thought her friend would have a fit. Sitting down, too, she filled Bev in on most of the story, leaving out the more intimate details. It was the first time in ages Stacy felt so alive, and she wanted to hug all her new feelings to herself.

When she came to the part about the sugar dousing her like so much snow on a Christmas tree, Bev clamped her hand over her mouth to stifle her giggles.

"I'm so glad I'm giving you a good laugh," Stacy said dryly before bursting into laughter.

When they finally calmed down, Bev studied Stacy carefully, then commented drolly, "Come clean, friend. There's more you're hiding from Mama. You've got that look in your eye and so does he." She clapped her hands together as if she'd discovered a great secret. "You're about to break out of the nunnery, aren't you?" she said gleefully. "Don't answer that. Just do it!"

Stacy blushed, confirming her friend's opinion. "There's a problem though."

"What problem?" Bev asked, suddenly concerned. "You're both healthy and unattached. He is, isn't he?"

Stacy explained all about the cardboard likeness in her home and why she'd purchased it.

"Still waters certainly run deep," Bev said. "I've got a whole new respect for you." But she agreed with Stacy. "Live competition is one thing, but no man wants to be fooled by a stiff. So why don't you just dump 'Harry' in the garbage?"

"I wish it were that simple," Stacy said. "For one thing, he's six feet tall with an iron bar down his back. He's mounted on a large heavy wooden base. I made such a fuss of needing it quickly, the man in the camera shop substituted heavy wood for the lighter base he'd run out of. Besides, that's only half my problem. What I really need is a logical excuse. I can't tell Kipp I did all this to make him think Harry was home on the weekends. He's still bitter because Felicia tricked him. If he knows the truth, I'll rank right up there with her."

"So tell him you used 'Harry' to ward off would-be burglars."

"Just on the weekends?" Stacy's brow shot up.

"No," she said. "It's all part of the same lie. You saw my reaction when I thought he'd lied to me. Besides, I could have gotten a guard dog to ward off burglars. At least a dog is there all week."

Bev cheerfully dismissed Stacy's fears. "You'll think of something. I have faith in you. Anyone with the ability to cook up a crazy scheme like yours should be able to cook up one last story."

"It's not so funny," Stacy said glumly when she saw the happy smile on Bev's face. "Quit beaming."

Bev's hands made a circular motion over her abdomen. "I'm beaming, my flighty friend, because I have some good news of my own. You're going to be an almost-aunt again. Isn't it wonderful? I'm positively ecstatic."

Stacy hugged and kissed her friend. Privately she was concerned for Bev. Her first pregnancy hadn't been easy.

"That's not all, Stacy," Bev said, her gray eyes dancing merrily.

"Don't tell me you're having twins?" Stacy eyed Bev's stomach.

Bev looked horrified. "No, you silly goose. The big joke is that I'm scheduled to model the bridal clothes at the annual fund-raising dinner for the hospital. It's all going to be very lah-de-dah posh at the country club in Morristown. Claudine's Bridal Shop is doing the show. They're going to choreograph it to be just like a mock wedding, complete with ceremony and groom. Naturally, Vito's been pressed into service as the groom. Poor guy. He's been going around the house saying it's a shotgun wedding. Isn't that crazy?" Bev finished with a laugh, "I'll be right in style. A pregnant bride."

"Do you think you'll be showing then? When is it?"

"No, I won't, and it's December twenty-seventh, right between Christmas and New Year's."

"You'll pull it off, Bev. Just take care of yourself and don't overdo."

On the drive home Stacy voiced her concern to Kipp. He told her of Vito's plans to hire a woman to help take care of Jeff so Bev would have plenty of rest.

Stacy asked Kipp to play some music and he switched on a tape. Melissa Manchester's sexy strains filled the car. Stacy was grateful she didn't have to make small talk. She was still trying to figure out her next step.

"We're home," Kipp said, startling her out of rehearsing her lines. He removed his hand from the steering wheel and turned to face her. In the reflected streetlamp his blue eyes, the color of the sea before a storm, burned into hers with an intensity that went straight to her core. He reached over, closing his hand on hers.

"Hey, your hands are freezing. It's not that cold outside," he said, and she wondered if all condemned liars shared a common nervous condition. He began to rub her fingers and she felt the warmth rush through her.

As if sensing her anxiety, he asked, "Will you be all right? Would you rather not come over?" There was an odd tone in his voice, as if he were afraid to hear her answer to him.

Stacy's heart catapulted into her stomach. Twinges of misgiving raced through her. She knew she was treading on dangerous ground. One way or another her decision would be irrevocable.

"No," she stammered, then, finding her resolve,

she said with more confidence, "No, I want to come. We need to talk."

"Stacy," he coaxed gently, "wouldn't it be easier if you just told me whatever it is now?"

"Kipp, I'd rather change into some comfortable clothes first," she said, easing her hand from his. Actually, she wanted more than anything to get her confession over with, but no matter how many times she considered her situation, she hadn't come up with a good excuse for "Harry."

Kipp looked at her soberly. Checking his watch, his deep voice filled the car's small chamber. "Fifteen minutes," he said, leaning across her to open her car door.

But as his arm brushed against her breasts, she felt as if an electric jolt passed from his body to hers.

"You really are freezing," he said softly. His hand cupped her chin. Applying a light pressure, he brought his face close to hers, but instead of kissing her, as she hoped he would, his warm lips grazed her throbbing temple. Running his thumb across her lips, he held her captive with the lightest of touches.

"Don't be long," he murmured huskily.

Once inside her house she was a flurry of motion. She rushed up the stairs. Flipping the switch on in her bedroom, she quickly slipped off her dress and high heels. Wearing only her blue teddy, she opened her closet and reached for a skirt. A loud crash suddenly filled the room. She jumped in fear. Her heart beat crazily.

"Oh, no!" she screamed, turning around toward the window. "Not again!"

The pesky spring-action curtain rod she'd recently purchased was cut a bit too short. It had been hanging by a wing and a prayer. It had already fallen down several times. She'd promised herself to buy another one but hadn't gotten around to it. What caused it to fall down tonight she couldn't guess and she didn't care. All she knew was she'd have to get "Harry" out of the brightly lit window. Without the protective curtain to mask him, he stood there for all to see. Still, the anticipation of dumping her security blanket was both exhilarating and anxiety-producing. If butterflies in the stomach could be rated on a scale of ten, hers rated a definite twelve.

"Harry," she announced, putting her arms around his waist to get into position to lift him, "it's time to get on with my life."

She took a step backward, expecting "Harry" to "waltz" away from the window with her. Nothing happened. "Harry" refused to budge!

She tried again. "He" balked.

"Listen, you," she fumed, her eyes narrowing at her adversary. "This is no time to proclaim your independence." She licked the beads of perspiration forming on her upper lip.

She changed tactics. Grunting, she tried to heave him up under his arms.

Obstinate, "Harry" remained glued to the floor.

"Don't you dare play this nonsense with me," she screamed. "Move!"

"Harry" smiled benevolently down at her and stayed put.

"You rat, I don't have time to play games."

She kicked him and hurt her toe. She rested her head for a moment on "Harry's" chest. Glancing downward, she spied the source of the problem. The heavy base was caught under the rug where some tacking had come loose.

She shimmied down his body. As she worked the base free, "Harry" began to tilt.

"Oh, no, you don't!" she wailed, standing up quickly to fling herself against him before he crashed through the window. She could see the headlines now: "Third Grade Schoolteacher Commits Suicide with Cardboard Likeness of Ex-Husband."

"Why doesn't anything every come easily where you're concerned?" she wailed, fighting gravity and perspiring now in earnest.

It took her another five minutes of grunting, grabbing, and spreading herself all over him to move the display to the other wall.

Breathing hard from all the exertion, she caught a glimpse of herself in the beveled mirror. Her hair was wild. Her face was beet-red. She raced into the bathroom to wash and to repair the damage. If anything else was going to happen to her, she didn't want it to be tonight. She'd had it!

From his darkened bedroom Kipp planned to set his telescope in the direction of Vega. Instead, his attention was drawn to the brightly lit room across the way. Where there once had been a curtain, now there was nothing.

He could hardly believe the scene unfolding before his eyes. Grabbing the telescope, he pressed his eyes so tightly against the lens, he thought his face would have permanent rim lines. All Stacy wore was the teddy he'd once seen on her bed. As he watched, his hopes for the evening came tumbling down.

He hadn't believed her when she told him Harry was home sleeping. But it was true. Harry was really home, in the flesh, accepting Stacy's adoration like a potentate accepting homage. So how could she be making a date to come over to his house?

He had been sure Stacy's marriage was in its final

throes. She couldn't have responded to him so passionately otherwise. Or could she? he wondered morosely.

He watched the unfolding tableau with a sinking feeling as Stacy placed her head on her husband's chest, her arms drawn tightly around his waist. Kipp cursed himself for the blind fool he was.

What a lousy detective he'd make! He'd misinterpreted all the clues because he wanted to. The medicine cabinet with only her things in it, the solitary toothbrush in the holder, Stacy's nervousness whenever Harry's name came up. He'd seen her room the night he'd run up for something to clean and dress her wounds. She'd left the closets open. All he'd seen were her things. He remembered being surprised by that. Later, he'd pieced this clue to the rest. Now, sitting there glumly in the dark, he realized that the clues he'd thought signaled a woman living alone were just so much nonsense. The kiss she'd shared with him earlier meant only one thing. Stacy enjoyed an extramarital fling.

She certainly didn't need his help, that much was clear. On the contrary, she could teach him a thing or two! Far from resisting Harry's embrace, she seemed to be in a frenzy of sexual activity. Kipp's mood plummeted as his plans for the evening collapsed into thin air.

He wiped his forehead and kept his eyes on the action. Far from being unhappy with her traveling spouse, Stacy was climbing all over him: hands, chest, the works! Dammit, didn't she have a shred of modesty? Decent women, he fumed in a jealous rage, did not slide up and down a man's body in full view of the neighborhood. If Stacy wanted to sell tickets to a girlie show, she couldn't give a better sneak preview.

The telescope gave him a front row seat. She was making love in front of the window! The next thing the brazen hussy would do, he thought, was to complete the act. How could he be so wrong about someone? Had the woman no shame? She was no better than Felicia. No, he took that back. At least Felicia had the good sense to keep the blinds drawn.

A light flashed in his brain. Now he understood. Stacy was a hot number. Who knew? Maybe she was a nymphomaniac. He'd told her he was divorced. Like an idiot he'd confessed to her how lonely he was. He'd shared intimate feelings with her. She knew he lived alone except for a dog. What could be safer? He'd played right into her hands. And what those hands were engaged in now drove his blood pressure up! She'd known he wanted her. Hell, he'd made it abundantly clear. He couldn't wait to get home.

She probably was going to suggest a little Monday-to-Friday tryst. Then, when lover boy came home from his travels needing sleep, she'd be the loving, understanding, sexually satisfied wife.

He wiped the steam from the scope's lens. Drawn like a magnet, he pressed his face back into position for some more torture. He felt empty, betrayed. Glowering, his face drawn into a furious knot, he saw Stacy move away, giving him his first really sharp view of her husband's features.

Kipp peered into the scope again. He focused it to a pinpoint sharpness. He wanted to see the man. After tonight he didn't intend ever to have anything more to do with her. He stared intently and blinked his eyes. Then he stared again. Stepping back, he shook his head. Something was drastically wrong. He peered into the scope again. He caught a glimpse of something round and shiny on Harry's arms. Carefully, he studied the gleaming objects. "What the hell!" He expelled his breath in disbelief. "Those are grommets!"

Slowly the fog of uncertainty lifted. Dumbfounded, he still had a hard time believing his eyes. Shaking his head, he stood up and threaded his fingers through his thick hair. No one would believe this in a million years, he thought in utter amazement. A surge of wild hope replaced rejection.

Harry, the loving husband who traveled from one continent to another, wasn't moving a muscle because he didn't have any!

Dear old Harry was catatonic!

Harry was stiff as a board!

Harry was a board!

Kipp threw himself down on the bed and howled. He laughed so hard he doubled up in pain. He laughed until the tears trickled from the corners of his eyes. What a woman!

A preposterous thought seeped into his mind and he stopped laughing abruptly. Why was Stacy making love to a piece of cardboard? The possibilities sifting through his mind were too sick. He grabbed the phone and dialed his psychiatrist friend, Ed Stein. Midnight or not, he needed help!

A sleepy growl greeted his hello. "Ed, wake up," Kipp shouted into the receiver. All he heard was a snore. "Are you up?"

"No, I'm not up. *Go away!*"

Frantic, Kipp yelled, "Ed, you're awake or you wouldn't be shouting. Tell Franny I'm sorry if I woke her up. This won't take much time. I need an answer—fast." Kipp heard a mumbling sound. Afraid his ex-college roommate from the Columbia University medical school would hang up, he rushed to ask, "Why would a woman make love to a cardboard dummy?" He didn't add the location. If it became necessary, he'd tell him that too.

A spate of healthy curse words sliced across the phone lines, stinging Kipp's ear. "Do you mean you've got the gall to get me up from a deep sleep to ask me a crazy question like that? Are you playing a game or are you into kinky sex partners? You notice, Kipp Palmer, I didn't have to ask who's calling."

"No speeches, Ed. Just answer the question!" Kipp glanced at his watch. He expected Stacy any minute. Pacing the length of his room, he wrapped the long cord around his wrist, symbolically tugging a response. "I'll owe you one, Ed. Answer the question."

"How the hell do I know?" Ed growled impatiently, awake now.

"You're a lot of help."

Hearing Ed sigh, Kipp waited tensely.

"All right, I'll make a deal with you. If you swear on a stack of Bibles to bother another psychiatrist in the future, you may call my secretary in the morning. I promise I'll see your young woman and her cardboard fetish. In fact, if it'll make her happier, she can bring all the cardboard she wants. I'll even show you how good I am to you. You can even bring Connie along. Then I can treat the whole nutty bunch of you." Ed Stein's cackling laughter ended Kipp's hopes for a medical interpretation. Ed really thought he was playing a joke on him.

"You stink, Stein. Don't ever need an operation! You hear?" Kipp slammed the receiver down, feeling more frustrated. He'd have to help Stacy as best as he could. He only hoped whatever he told her made sense. Shooting a last look across the way, he noticed the lights were now out in Stacy's room. He hurried down the stairs to light the fire in the living room fireplace. He wasn't sure how to proceed. Nothing in the medical books remotely prepared him for this.

He'd fallen head over heels in love with a bonafide kook!

Stacy stood quietly in the middle of the living room while Kipp hung up her navy pea jacket. "Harry's" final hurrah had made her a half hour late. Considering the hour, she supposed she should have called to postpone their meeting, but supposing and doing didn't always follow a set pattern with Stacy. Kipp had been more than understanding when she rang the bell. Apart from telling her how lovely she looked, he'd asked her no questions.

She felt inexplicably shy. She'd thought she'd come over, tell Kipp directly about her divorce, and let him make the next move. Now, as she glanced around the room, she suddenly felt like fleeing. The room was too cozy, the lights too dim, the couch too invitingly large and cushiony, the carpeting too plush. It looked like the expensively furnished den of a bachelor on the prowl.

She sought refuge in examining a mahogany side table. Her eyes scanned its highly polished surface and the exquisite pitcher set on a scrolled silver tray in the center. She couldn't resist examining the delicate china decorated with an overall pattern of small violets. Turning it over, she read the distinctive signature of Limoges. She glanced up to find Kipp quietly studying her.

"Are you interested in antiques, Stacy?"

"I don't know too much about them," she answered honestly. Kipp stood beside her.

He put his hand on her shoulder, smiled encouragingly, and said, "Neither do I. I just buy what I like when I happen to come across it. Some people call it eclectic collecting, I think. That's a fancy way of saying a novice can enjoy beautiful objects too. When I purchased this table it was pure luck. I happened to be driving by a church in Chester which was scheduled for demolition. The parishioners were having a lawn sale, so I stopped the car and spoke with Father Maroney and came away with this."

"It's a refectory table, isn't it?" she asked, pretending to examine it more closely, yet conscious of Kipp's warm hand playing on her skin. A thrill of desire shot through her and she swallowed hard to avert her eyes from his penetrating gaze.

"Yes," he answered, moving a step closer to stroke his hand up and down her arm. Tingling, she watched his mouth, forcing herself to concentrate on his explanation.

"Closed," he said, dipping his head to breathe near her cheek, "it's twenty-four inches wide." Stacy unconsciously moved her cheek toward his lips, sighing in soft satisfaction as he kissed her cheek. His lips against her skin, he continued. "It separates by pulling the opposite sides away to allow the inserted board to rise up flush to the surface of the table. It's a perfect fit," he said, his lips seeking the corner of her mouth. "Sometimes," he murmured, sliding his lips toward her ear, and she felt her insides turn to jelly, "things don't fit perfectly; they're mismatched, wouldn't you agree?"

"Of course," she answered, inanely wondering what the subject was. She was putty in his arms. His warm breath feathered her ear as she inhaled the masculine fragrance of Paco Rabanne.

"There isn't a nail in this beauty." Kipp's hand moved to caress the column of her neck. His fingers massaged its base hypnotically. "Open, it's forty inches wide. I figure wherever I live, the table will fit. But you didn't come over here to discuss my antiques, did you?" he whispered, pressing a kiss to the base of her neck just before he turned her around in his arms.

Kipp's blue eyes caressing her face made her feel weak. "How about a drink?" he asked, diverting her attention from the cleft in his chin. "I think we could both use some wine, don't you?"

She needed to clear her head. Two minutes with him and she fogged up completely. Gratefully, she accepted the glass of white wine. "Where's Connie?" she asked, running out of alternate conversations.

"In the basement."

"The basement? Why?" she asked, thinking it odd that Kipp would confine Connie in a cold, damp cellar.

"Don't feel so sorry for the monster," he said cryptically. "The basement in this house is fully furnished, warm, and carpeted. You've met Connie. There's no telling what that hound will do. I just thought you'd find it easier to talk without distractions. Come over here and sit down."

He surprised her by leading her past the couch and indicating she sit in one of two facing wing chairs in front of the fireplace. He sat down, crossed his legs, took another sip of his wine, and placed the wineglass on a small Queen Anne table near the chair.

He gave her his full attention. "All right, Stacy, I'm listening. I think we've run out of small talk, don't you?"

She nodded. *Let me do this right*, she prayed. Glad to have something to hide her nervousness, she clasped the glass in her hand tightly. "Kipp, I've thought about how I was going to tell you this all evening. I guess there's no better way than to plunge right in."

"Stacy, I'm not an ogre. I'd never hurt you. Plunge."

Stacy looked at him, the silent plea for understanding written on her face. "You're not the only one who's divorced, Kipp. I am too. I have been since before you and I met." There, she said it. She waited for him to call her a liar, to ask why she didn't tell him earlier at Bev's house. To her infinite relief his expression seemed to hold no recriminations, only concern. He didn't even once mention Cardboard Harry!

He left his chair and dropped down on the carpet beside her. He removed the glass from her hand and, turning for a moment, reached backward to place it on the table near his.

"And all that business about racing back and forth to Kennedy Airport—?"

"Wasn't true," she said in a small voice.

"The Bombay flu?" She didn't see his mouth twitching.

"I made it up." Stacy sat up straight in her chair, clasping her hands.

"No wonder I never heard of it. Why?"

"Why not?" she said, defending herself. "You let me think you were married to Millie. At least I didn't try palming off an excuse like that. Your own sister, for goodness' sake!"

"Touché."

"Is that all you have to say?" she asked, clearly thankful he didn't refer to the rest of her duplicity.

"No. Right from the beginning I had the feeling your marriage was in trouble. I didn't know you were divorced. Frankly, I'm delighted. I thought I'd have to wait on the sidelines until you made up your mind about your marriage. Tell me about Harry. I want to understand."

She couldn't believe it. Kipp was making it so easy for her. Suddenly she wanted to tell him everything, to share the months of pain and humiliation she'd suffered. "We were married young," she began. "I fell in love with him in high school. He didn't see me for dust then. He was older and the big letter man on campus. Later I went to the same college he did. When he noticed me, I was thrilled. My parents and Bev tried to tell me I should be dating others, too, but I wouldn't listen."

"Where are your parents? Do they live around here?"

"No. They're snowbirds now. They're both retired teachers, and they've moved to Clearwater Beach in Florida."

"Go on," he urged.

"After we were married I discovered little disturbing things about Harry that I had been too blind to see before. One of us was growing up, and it was me." She made no attempt to quell the tears forming in her eyes. For the first time in a long time she felt as if she were cleansing herself of all the hurt.

"And then what?" Kipp asked, knowing she was going through a catharsis. There'd be time later for them. First, he needed to find out why she still didn't seem able to let go, why she still felt the need to keep Harry with her, if only through a likeness. He handed her the glass of wine.

"He left me for greener pastures. Literally. Mona is rich. I'm not. Harry spent a lot of money on designer labels. He seemed to think it went with the territory. He used to brag that his clients were impressed by a show of wealth."

"What does Harry do?" Kipp asked quietly.

"That's the sad part," she said, and seemed to

turn inward. "He's very talented in sales and very charming, but he changed jobs often. The problem was he couldn't seem to settle down. He wanted everything fast. Money went out like water. I earned extra money by tutoring. Also, I like to write children's stories, but Harry always said it was a waste of time. So I stopped. In the end, I was too blind to know what was going on right under my nose." She sniffed and reached for the tissue Kipp pressed into her hand. "Do you know," she said, and hiccupped on a sob, thinking about her Dr. Jerome and Manuela, "it was only recently I began to write again?" She stopped short of blurting out to Kipp he was the real star of her story.

"Good for you, Stacy. I think that's wonderful." He waited for a moment while she composed herself. Then he gently probed for the information uppermost in his mind. "Who else knows about your divorce?"

"No one. Just my immediate family and Bev and Vito."

Kipp was plainly surprised. "You mean the people you work with think you're still married?" When she nodded, he said, "You've put yourself under a tremendous strain. You must have loved Harry very much."

"I did," she said, missing the pained expression on Kipp's face.

"Stacy, I want you to follow very closely what I'm about to say." Kipp stood up, towering over her, and handed her the wineglass. Obediently, she sipped from it while her eyes remained glued to the serious expression on his face. He picked up a poker and rearranged the log in the fireplace. He stared into the embers. Taking a deep breath, he wished he had a telepathic tie-in to Ed Stein's brain.

"You've been through a hellish experience at a young age. Sometimes it's easier for the mind to deny rather than accept awful experiences. It's a kind of shock, a trauma to the system. Do you follow what I'm saying?"

"Not really," she admitted. "What am I denying? Do you mean by my not telling the people I work with about my divorce, I'm denying it really happened?"

"Something like that. Stacy, some people hang on to lost loves. It's quite common when a loved one dies. Sometimes it's impossible for people to clean out a beloved person's belongings. You've heard of people who keep their first spouse's pictures all over the house even after they've remarried, haven't you?"

"I don't have Harry's pictures all over the house," she protested innocently. "I don't have anything of his. No, that's not exactly true," she said, and Kipp waited with baited breath. "There's some junk in the attic. I hate going up there because it makes me sneeze."

Kipp felt as if he were losing the most important battle of his life. If he couldn't get her to own up that Harry, dead or alive, was still important in her life, how could she come to terms with the future? She was still living in the past. What hope was there for him? Desperate, he said, "There is something of Harry you can't part with."

Stacy saw the conflicting emotions on Kipp's face. She racked her brain. "Harry" wasn't in the house the night she hurt her toe. That was the only time until tonight he'd have had a chance to really see . . . The curtain rod! The lights! The window! So that was the reason she was being psychoanalyzed. She lowered her head. The tears streamed from her eyes as her head shook back and forth, her body racked by spasms.

Kipp was by her side instantly. He put his arms around her. She hid her face against his chest. "Honey, I'm sorry. Forgive me. I didn't mean to upset you. All I wanted to do was help you come to terms with the truth so there'd be a chance for us. I asked Ed for help, but he—"

"Ed? Isn't he . . . You mean," she said, convulsing so hard, her body shook in earnest, "you asked the dog's psychiatrist to help me. Oh, you big, wonderful dope. I'm not crying, I'm laughing."

"Laughing!" Kipp's astonishment matched hers as he pulled her hands down from her face. He stepped back. "You *are* laughing," he cried in amazement.

"Were you upstairs in your room right after we came home tonight?" she asked, reaching up to run her fingers over his cheek. When he nodded, she cupped his face between her hands. "What you saw tonight, my precious dope, was a piece of cardboard."

"I know that," he said, desperate for understanding. "You know that?"

"Of course I do," he said. "What was it doing in your room?"

"It was there because of you," she admitted, wiping her eyes.

"Me?" Thoroughly confused, he was beginning to get the idea he needed Ed more than ever.

"To keep you out of my hair, you big lug. I needed you to think Harry was home, didn't I? You were always there wherever I turned."

"What?"

"That was before I wanted you in my hair, of course," she said, kissing the cleft in his chin that had been driving her crazy.

Kipp gripped her by the arms. "Are you saying

you're not a weirdo after all? This was just another one of your tricks?"

"I solemnly swear I'm not a weirdo after all. It worked, didn't it?" she said, kissing the pout off his lips.

"No, it didn't." He gently pushed her away.

"What do you mean?"

"I mean," he said, his voice so low it sounded as if he growled, "it's going to take a hell of a lot more than just a kiss to get me in a better frame of mind."

"Like what?" she asked, dropping her lashes demurely.

"Oh, no, Ms. Jump-to-Conclusions Conklin, no more tricks. Open your eyes. I want you to see exactly what's coming to you." He pulled her into his arms, kissing her until she was breathless.

"Now what?" she whispered, loving the feel of his lips on hers.

"Guess," he said as he lifted her in his arms to carry her upstairs to his bedroom.

Seven

Kipp carried Stacy up the stairs and strode down the hall. As he entered his room she caught a quick impression of a wall of shelves filled with books and an entertainment center opposite a window. In front of the window there was a telescope mounted on a tripod base.

The massive bed reminded her of him. Made of rock-strong mahogany, it was thoroughly masculine even to the brown geometric-print spread that he was hurriedly pulling to the foot of the bed.

A self-conscious smile darted past her lips and faded. Kipp leaned forward, one arm trapping her slim form while his other hand tilted up her face.

"Kiss me," he said huskily.

Her arms took on a life of their own as they reached behind his neck to draw his face down to hers. In what suddenly seemed the most natural of acts, her fingers curled in his thick hair, threading through its rich lushness to knead his skull in a lover's caress.

He met her halfway, wrapping one arm around

her. He pulled her securely against his chest and she felt the heavy thrumming of his heart match her own. With his other hand he cupped her head in his broad palm. Impulsively, her fingers crept down to test the texture of his beard.

He warmly, slowly, explored the outline of her lips with his tongue. He took her bottom lip between his teeth and tugged gently. Lightly nipping, stroking, rubbing sensuously across its contoured shape from side to side, he worked on her upper lip.

Imitating his lead, Stacy's tongue traced the firm outline of his lips, teasing him with tiny darting movements. Then he opened his mouth and his tongue delved deeply into hers. Boldly, the warm wet tip of her tongue began an intense exploration of its own. Her heart tripped crazily as the demands of the kiss grew hotter and harder. Kipp played her mouth as a virtuoso plays a musical instrument. Stacy felt as if a thousand tiny cymbals were clashing along the length of her spine.

When at last the drugging kiss ended, her eyelids fluttered open and she looked into his eyes. It was obvious the kiss had affected him as deeply as it had her. Their breaths were harsh and raspy, forming short puffs of air. She moaned and moved over to give him room between her and the edge of the bed. He took a deep breath, as if willing himself to slow down.

Massaging the column of her neck with his finger-tips, he lightly kissed the tip of her nose. Instead of joining her on the bed, he said in a voice full of sexual innuendo, "Not yet, my cute little conniver. I haven't finished paying you back for all the nights of hell you've put me through. A cardboard dummy, huh! With grommets no less! I'll show you what a live man can do."

Her eyes widened. Smiling languorously, she crooked her little finger. With a hint of mystery playing over her face, she accepted his challenge. In her best imitation of Mae West, she beckoned him on. "Masochist," she whispered, and privately he thought she was right.

"You won't need this," he said as he unzipped the placket of her skirt. He lifted her hips, dropped a kiss below her waistband, then quickly removed the beige skirt. She teasingly rocked her torso from side to side.

She wasn't wearing a slip. "You don't play fair, do you?"

Deftly he unbuttoned the top button of her silk blouse. Blowing lightly, he pressed his lips to her creamy skin. As he kissed her, she felt his tongue sear her skin, igniting the flames of passion. Receiving her first delightful lesson in his revenge, she shivered.

His eyes stayed on her while his fingers found the second button and quickly opened it. He dipped his head, his lips and tongue grazing the valley between her breasts, nuzzling her creamy flesh. He plied her with dozens of soft kisses, rapidly inspiring her to moan with pleasure.

He laughed softly and opened still another button, exposing the lacy top of her silk teddy. His eyes feasted on her gently heaving breasts beneath the slinky silk lingerie.

"You're not wearing a bra either," he muttered thickly.

Glorying in her femininity, Stacy watched Kipp's hands reverently cup her small breasts, pushing them higher with his palms. Her eyes grew heavy-lidded under the slow, intoxicating motion of his thumb and his forefinger on her taut nipple. The calculated slowness caused an intense heat between her thighs. He leaned down again and her fingers sliced through his hair. She whimpered as his lips and tongue brushed the ripe fullness of her bosom through the thin silk barrier.

The devastating combination of the slightly abrasive texture of his chin and the hot wet slippery silk on her bare nipples took her breath away. With infinite tenderness his mouth took her nipple between his teeth. He rolled his tongue around the hard nub. Stacy whimpered softly. Instinctively, she arched closer as her sensitive breasts ached to be free of the hampering cloth.

He drew in a shallow breath, slipped the narrow shoulder straps from her arms, and kissed the pulsing hollow at the base of her neck. She purred and cooed and sighed softly.

"Easy, honey," he crooned, dropping a kiss on her soft round breast. When he lifted her hand, pretending to examine some invisible spot on her palm, Stacy drew a deep calming breath.

The short reprieve ended as he circled her palm with his tongue. Her eyes shot open. A strong shudder rolled through her and he chuckled in satisfaction. She gasped as he drew her pinkie into his hot, moist mouth, sucking and moving it slowly up and down. He treated each of her fingers to the same unhurried leisurely punishment until Stacy's involuntary moan made him stop.

He took a torturously slow route as he undressed her. He rained kisses down her rib cage and past her narrow waist. The blue teddy sailed through the air, landing on the floor near the foot of the bed. She lay unashamedly naked before him.

She could feel the steamy tension coil deep in her belly like a taut spring. Her head spun. Her entire world was centered on the perimeters of the bed. Nothing else mattered.

Impatiently, needing to feel him, too, she placed her hands under his shirt, tugging it free from the waistband of his pants. "How long are you planning to keep this up?" she gasped, letting her fingers spread across his chest. She saw him struggle with his answer.

"Patience," he said huskily, "I just want to make sure you don't play any more of your tricks on me."

"Oh, I don't know." She gulped. "You have such an interesting way of making the punishment fit the crime."

He kissed the sensitive lobe of her ear. She sighed and the throaty purr in her voice answered his need to give her pleasure.

Finally, when he knew he was reaching the end of his tether, he eased himself away from her. "Had enough?" he teased, but his voice was strained.

Sure in the knowledge she was going to win either way, she flashed him a saucy smile. Batting her lashes, she answered coyly, "Thank you very much. I think I'll go home now."

"Don't even try it," he said.

"What will you do?" she asked, her fingers making a slow foray into the dark mat of hair on his chest.

"This."

In a flash he rolled on top of her, pulling her over to his side. He threw his long leg over her hip to prevent her from moving. As Kipp drank in her beauty, all his pent-up yearnings, the feelings he'd buried so deeply inside him, struggled to the surface, and he pressed himself so closely to her that no space existed between them. The texture of her creamy skin, the soft curves beneath his roaming hand, elated him.

Stacy felt safe with the knowledge that Kipp would be the second man in her life to know her intimately.

"The first time I saw you I wanted to do this," he whispered against her lips. "You almost drove me crazy standing in front of me near the sink the day you spilled the sugar."

Stacy's heart pounded furiously. She thought she'd die if she couldn't touch him as he was touching her. "Take off your clothes," she demanded, not knowing how much more of this she could take.

"Help me," he murmured, gladly putting an end to the game.

Together their hands worked quickly. She helped him to shed his slacks which joined her skirt, blouse, and teddy on the floor. In a deft motion his underwear was removed, then his socks, and they, too, landed on the heap on the floor.

"You're beautiful," she said softly, letting her eyes roam over his trim body.

"That's my line," he said, feathering kisses along her jaw and in the hollow behind her ear until she squirmed.

"You are beautiful, you know. And soft and so desirable it makes my heart bang against the walls of my chest." He gathered her back into his arms, holding her while their hearts raced. His fingers left a trail of fire wherever they touched.

He traced the shape of her breasts, then feathered downward, stopping to squeeze her narrow waist gently before opening his palm and circling her abdomen. When his fingers brushed the delicate skin along the insides of her thighs, she moaned and turned, writhing against him. Slipping lower, his hand caressed her. His fingers found the sensitive pulse of her womanhood which sprang to life beneath his touch. Where his fingers left, his lips paid homage until Stacy felt as if she were a quivering mass of explosive need.

Panting unevenly, she closed her eyes. She wanted to give him the same pleasure he was giving her. Her hands reached for him. She gave in to her own quest.

"That's right," he coaxed her, his voice tight with his own desire. Her fingers mimicked his, giving him the same sweet torture he'd given her. Her lips tugged at the hard nipples buried in his chest hair.

His fingers tangled with her hair, smoothing it away from her face so he could watch her. He said her name softly, wonderingly, repeating it as a chant. He stilled her hand and quickly maneuvered her body beneath his. Rising, he nudged his leg between hers, opening her thighs for him. Urgently, he lifted her hips away from the mattress.

Through half-closed eyes she saw his face above hers, heard his words of encouragement. Then, as she felt the full force of his entry, she gasped at the wonder of it.

He stopped, and she saw the strain on his face, the tenseness in his elbows. "Stacy, am I hurting you?"

"No," she said, moving instinctively with him.

The hungering, passionate sounds he made pierced her with such longing and tenderness she was shaken. As he moved inside her, he whispered love words in her ear.

Once again his lips clung to hers as he timed his movements to make sure she was with him. She gave her body up to him completely, indulging in a lusty, sensuous passion. Her head lolled from side to side on the pillow. Clinging to him, her fingers dug into his shoulders. She could feel his hot breath mingling with her own. Her body felt ready to explode.

"Kipp, I . . . I don't know how much more I can stand."

"Let it go, darling. Let it go." She felt his rhythm change, increasing in tempo, and she tightened her legs around him.

His words released a spasm of electrifying emotion. A ray of moonlight spilled through the open window, lighting his face. He was a powerful, magnificent man capable of carrying her through the heavens. He kissed her hungrily, capturing her outpouring of searing pleasure. And when they came back to earth locked in each other's arms and the shock waves receded, Kipp rolled off her and fiercely pulled her into the nest of his body.

He was the first to break the silence.

"Whew, lady," he said, kissing her tenderly, "you're nothing short of magnificent."

Filled with the wonder of their union, Stacy couldn't find adequate words. Feebly, she said, "That was some punishment you dished out."

"If I weren't so tired," he said contentedly, "I'd teach you another lesson."

"Promises, promises," she whispered drowsily.

Several hours later Kipp listened to the quiet, even breathing of the woman curled up beside him. Assailed by a nagging feeling of doubt, he'd slept only a short time. Instead of being ecstatically happy, he was worried.

He'd been shocked to learn Stacy kept her divorce a secret. It also made him wonder whether she had entertained private hopes for a reconciliation with her ex-husband. Stranger things had been known to happen. People remarried their exes all the time. Hadn't she'd told him Harry was her first love? In her case that love started all the way back in high school. And from the sound of what she'd said to him, Harry was a very powerful first love.

If he'd had any sense at all last night, he would have listened to her story, asked her for a date, and steered her back home. Then he'd have been able to marshal his own feelings for her instead of falling like a ton of bricks.

He'd never known a woman as passionately giving or as much fun to be with as Stacy. As he lay there with his glum thoughts, he decided Harry had to be the biggest idiot of all time. How Harry could trade Stacy for money when he already had the most price-less gift in the world was beyond Kipp's comprehen-sion. In either case, she needed time to heal before she could make a serious commitment to anyone, including him.

What worried him the most was the possibility that she might be using him as a replacement for Harry while she got her self-confidence back. She might not even be aware she was doing this, but the possibility existed.

On the other hand, he wasn't interested in casual sex with her. If he didn't know it before, last night clinched it. She meant so much to him. Regardless of whether his fears held credence or not, it was much too soon for him to tell her how he felt. If anything, it might scare her away.

"You can't push the stages of recovery," Ed had told him one particularly bad day. "It's like grieving for the dead, except death is final. Divorce, believe it or not, drags out the recovery process, especially if you're the partner receiving the kick in the back-side!" As Kipp placed his palm on Stacy's cute little rump, he acknowledged that she had indeed received a very large kick.

Stacy stirred in her sleep. Her arm was draped along his thigh; her back was curled up against his chest, her womanly body shaping itself to his. She sighed and her hand slipped down to rest naturally near his manhood. His noble second thoughts were buried as her fingers reached him.

She was tantalizing him, innocently fanning his passions while she slept. She bent her leg back, tucking it between his, and she moved her body closer to his to use him for a blanket. She sighed again, and he felt her warm breath on the palm of his hand. Now what was he supposed to do? After all his heroic intentions, he felt his control slipping again.

His hands itched to do something. He settled for wedging one hand between her back and his chest. His fingers explored the small bones along her spine. She was so finely built. He was filled with an urge to protect her, but he also knew he had to protect himself. He'd been burned once. He couldn't go through it again.

He heard her murmur something in her sleep and he tilted his head, trying unsuccessfully to catch her words. He smoothed the hair away from her forehead and kissed her lightly. She sighed and fell back into a deep sleep.

Stacy readjusted herself against him with another of her little shoves. What was a man to do in the face of such manuevers? He groaned and tried to open a space between them. Each time he carefully tried to move away, she followed. It was as if her body were bound to his, seeking him out in spite of new obstacles. Even asleep the little minx managed to torment him.

Then he heard her slight giggle. "You little tease," he said, swatting her rump playfully. "Have you no shame? All this time you've been awake and purposely driving me out of my mind. And here I thought I was being so kind letting you get your beauty rest. Well, let's see how you like this." He growled, locking her securely with his hip.

Stacy laughed in mock concern. "What are you going to do?"

"I'm going to make you cry uncle, my sweet little vixen."

In the next few minutes he was all over her, igniting sparks and fiery trails. He nipped at her earlobe, kissed her neck, and breathed whispery words of sex play in her ear. She wanted to turn around, tried to turn around, but he continued to hold her captive. She felt as if all the exquisite nerves in her body were centered wherever he touched her. And when his fingers slid into the core of her being and began to stroke and circle, she felt as if she'd go mad with pleasure.

"All right, my little witch, are you ready to say uncle?"

"Never." She laughed, but it sounded more like a plea.

"Say it." He groaned, but it sounded more like begging.

"I'll tickle you!"

"Uncle . . ." she squeaked as Kipp grunted in satisfaction. "Uncle . . . anything."

He released her only for the time it took to turn her around. Pinning her to the mattress, he looked deeply into her eyes and she saw the raw passion once again darken their hue. The teasing stopped. Together they wondered at the beauty of the other's form. Bringing her back into the circle of his arms, he spoke softly, reverently. They kissed and touched to give each other pleasure.

Emboldened by a new feeling of freedom, Stacy became the aggressor. Her blond hair caped their faces as she leaned down to find his waiting lips. Her hands held him by the shoulders. Her legs locked tightly to his sides. He guided her along the journey, moving in unison with her. When he felt the tightening of her muscles and saw her arch her head back, he joined her in his own final crescendo.

In the pinkening sky that heralded the dawn of another day, they transcended time, transcended space, reaching heights of ecstasy neither had ever found before.

With a gentle breeze fanning the sheets covering them, Kipp drew Stacy to him. He cradled her back to his chest and settled one hand on her breast. With the other he felt the slight roundness of her tummy and marveled briefly at the miracle of a woman's body. He couldn't help but think what a wonderful mother Stacy would make. The thought triggered the knowledge that he hadn't used anything to protect her. *Smart doctor*, he scolded himself. *You're nothing more than a fool.* He hadn't asked her if she was on the pill.

"Stacy?"

"Mmm?" she murmured drowsily.

"This may be like closing the barn door after the horse got out, but were you using anything to protect yourself?"

"There's no problem, Kipp," she said easily. "The doctor didn't want me to go off the pill because it messed up my periods . . . Kipp?"

"Mmm?"

"How long have you had that telescope?"

"Why do you ask?"

"Because it's pointed at my bedroom. I could have you arrested for being a Peeping Tom."

His chuckle rumbled against her skin. "Should I call the police now? They'd be very interested in taking down your testimony."

"On second thought, shut up and go to sleep."

"I thought you'd see things my way," he said, getting in the last word.

Stacy stood by the bed studying the sleeping form of the man with whom she'd spent the night. Correction, she thought quickly, the man who'd made love to her through much of the night.

They were really strangers, she thought dispassionately. True, they'd made love and it was the most wonderful experience of her life, but how much did they really know about each other? If circumstances had been different and they'd met before either of them had married, would they have been drawn to each other? Or was it just loneliness that sparked the kind of night they'd spent together?

A part of her already knew some of the answers. Sex, as great as it was, wasn't enough. She'd once thought she had everything. Now she realized she'd had a husband she'd always loved more than he ever loved her.

In her newfound wisdom Stacy realized that the Monas of the world didn't just steal husbands. There was more to it than that. She'd been fooling herself thinking her marriage had gone sour because of Mona.

She'd had good sex with Harry. It just wasn't great sex. She realized that now after spending the night with a lusty lover who'd shown her things about her own body she hadn't known. So why couldn't she feel like the liberated woman she professed to be?

As she agonized over the answers to her own questions, she continued to gaze down at Kipp. He had fallen into a deep sleep. The covers were angled low across his hips, exposing one tightly muscled thigh and long leg.

Naked herself, she'd watch the steady, even rise of his broad chest and remembered the sound of his heartbeat thrumping in her ear. Her eyes made a slow revolution over his body, beginning with his powerful shoulders and his upper arms. *He looks more like a football player than a doctor*, she decided. His biceps bulged. She wondered if he lifted weights. Smiling to herself, she concluded rather haughtily that Kipp could best almost anyone in a fight. Except, she thought, the kind they had had last night.

His arms, she noted clinically, were incredibly long, perfect for his body and for wrapping themselves around hers. The hair on his forearms grew in a light dusting to his wrists, where it stopped abruptly in a trimmed, neat collar above his hands. Delicate yet large, it was his hands that reminded her of doctor's hands.

His face looked almost boyish. Only the cleft in his chin gave the hint of humor that was so much a part of his personality.

He was a great big, sexy man, she thought, and wondered why Felicia hadn't been satisfied to spend the rest of her days and nights with him.

The morning sun rose higher over the eastern sky. She should be going home. Home. Next door and a million miles away. If she were smart, she wouldn't make too much of last night. Kipp wasn't looking for a commitment. It was just as well. Everything was happening too fast for her. She trudged into the bathroom, picking up her clothes as she went.

She washed quickly and rinsed her face with cold water. She looked in the mirror and saw the slight pinkish hue on her skin where he'd kissed her over and over.

Tentatively, she traced the contours of her lips with her forefinger. They were slightly puffy, testimony to being kissed relentlessly.

Her hair was messy from Kipp's fingers and she quickly threaded her fingers through it. She looked, she thought, exactly like a woman who had spent the night doing exactly what she had been doing.

She dressed quietly so as not to disturb Kipp. She'd never spent the night with anyone but Harry, and she didn't know what to do anyway.

She tiptoed past the bed, reached the door, and put her hand on the knob, turning it ever so slightly. Expelling her breath, she put one foot on the other side of the doorsill, careful not to make any noise. Kipp's angry voice sliced through the room as he jumped out of bed and headed straight for her.

"And just where the hell do you think you're going?"

Eight

Stacy froze. Her heart was hammering so loudly, she thought it would burst.

Kipp was an awesome sight, glaring down at her from his towering height. A lock of hair fell over his forehead and he absentmindedly pushed it away. His gaze swung to her tightly buttoned blouse and he uttered an oath under his breath. He shook his head in an obvious attempt to control his frustration.

"I'm sorry, Stacy," he said when she flinched. "I didn't mean to frighten you just then." He added hastily, "Wait a minute. Let me put something on and we can talk."

A stab of warmth flooded her cheeks as she watched him reach down to the pile of his clothing scattered on the floor and perform the simple ritual of donning his pants. He slipped on his T-shirt and turned to her, his blue eyes hard and questioning.

"This isn't the way I pictured the morning after," he said wryly. "Where were you going?"

Tears scalded her eyes. She rapidly blinked them

away. "Can we go downstairs, please?" she said finally.

"Of course."

Kipp's hand extended in the direction of the door for her to precede him. With a quick self-conscious glance at the rumpled sheets on the bed in the background, she turned and left the room.

Bypassing the comfort of the living room, he led her to the kitchen and drew back the blinds to let the morning sun stream in.

"I think we can both use a cup of coffee, don't you?" he asked.

Stacy withdrew into a silent shell. She watched as Kipp set about fixing the coffee. As he crouched down on his haunches to get an unopened can of coffee from a low cabinet, she tried to remain unaffected by the sight of his hard muscular thighs in the snugly fitting jeans or the way his muscles strained the fabric of his shirt. His hair was disheveled. There was a faint shadow of beard on his face. He'd never looked handsomer to her. And when he turned and found her staring at him, a muscle worked in his jaw. Their eyes locked, holding her motionless for an instant. They waited in silence for the coffee maker to work. Then Kipp filled two mugs and brought the steaming coffee over to the table. Pulling out a chair for himself, he sat down, looking grim.

"All right, Stacy, why did you get cold feet? What happened between last night and this morning? You gave me every indication of a woman enjoying herself as much as I did, yet now you act like Cinderella running away at the stroke of midnight."

Stacy bristled. Trust a man to be so boorish. Even if his account were accurate, he didn't have to sit there throwing it up in her face!

Then why did she feel the heavy thud of her heart, the rush of adrenaline? She knew the answer. The pull of his blue eyes urged her to tell the truth.

"Kipp," she stammered, trying to make him understand what she still didn't fully understand herself, "I . . . I wasn't running away."

"No? You sure could've fooled me. What do you call it? You're sitting there all uptight, Miss Priss. You didn't have to try to sneak out without so much as a good-bye. Or were you going to leave me a note propped on the kitchen table beside a bag of doughnuts?"

"How could you say such a thing?" she snapped.

"Then who the hell were you running away from? Yourself?"

"What do you mean by that?" she hurled back at him. But she knew precisely what he meant, and it hurt. It hurt to be so transparent. Nervously, she reached for the Lucite holder, plucked a napkin, and unconsciously shredded it on the table.

Kipp watched as the small mound of white paper became higher. When Stacy started on a second napkin, he grabbed it out of her hand, impatiently balling the napkin in his fist.

"Oh, hell, I didn't mean to fly off the handle," he said when he saw her bite her trembling bottom lip. He took a gulp of his coffee. "I thought we'd gotten along so well. Why, Stacy?" he repeated in a low, strained voice, but his eyes had lost their icy rebuke.

"I'm repeating myself," he declared gruffly. "Go on home if you want to. I won't give you a hard time."

The pain she'd caused him was apparent in the hurt in his eyes and his taut features. She felt she owed him some explanation. She couldn't let it end this way, not when none of her actions were his fault.

"Last night . . . last night was . . ." She struggled for the words.

His eyes scanned her body as he helped her finish the sentence. "Wonderful," he supplied gently.

She felt the color rise in her cheeks. It was wonderful, too wonderful to pin her hopes on. Too wonderful to weave false dreams on.

"I . . . you . . . us. Oh, dear, I'm not very good at this." She lifted the mug to her lips, but her hands shook and the mug clattered down on the table.

A warning signal went off in Kipp's head. He should have known immediately. Hadn't he worried something like this would happen? It did. A lot sooner than he'd expected. That's what surprised him. Ed Stein had once warned him about the fragility of relationships following a divorce. "They very rarely get off to a good start," he'd cautioned.

At the time Kipp wasn't interested in the free advice his friend offered along with the luncheon the two were having. For the first year following his divorce from Felicia, Kipp kept his contacts with the opposite sex brief and nonbinding. It was a case of satisfying the call of nature and nothing more.

Now, worried he'd entered Stacy's life too soon anyway, he'd compounded the problem with his bullying. Damn him for being a first class fool!

The diagnosis was simple.

Stacy was quite literally scared out of her wits!

The grim line of his mouth softened as his long fingers reached across the table. His hands curled over hers for an instant, then backed away. It was enough. The tiny lifeline of compassion was all she seemed to need. Resolutely, she lifted her eyes. A small smile played at the corners of her mouth and dashed away as she strove to explain.

"Kipp, I've made one serious mistake in my life. I know I gave you the wrong impression last night—"

"The only impression you gave me last night was one of beauty and wonder."

She felt herself blush as she bravely went on with her explanation. "It sounds stupid and childish coming from a grown woman who's been married and divorced, but I'm not ready to jump into the fire again, not this soon. I thought I could, but it's all too fast for me. Couldn't we take this slower? Or maybe you want time to reconsider the wisdom of getting involved?"

"Meaning you do?" he queried softly.

"Meaning I think it would be better all around."

It was a while before he answered. "I agree, but with certain restrictions."

Stacy stared at Kipp in disbelief. Not two seconds ago he was harping at her for running out on him. His conditional agreement threw her for a loop. She wondered if his quasi-acquiescence was merely a defense for a bruised male ego.

"You do?" she asked cautiously.

"Let's just say I can see your point of view. Don't forget, we're kindred spirits."

"We are?"

"Stacy, a few minutes ago I was giving a pretty good imitation of an idiot. Forgive me, but after we made love last night I wanted to wake up with you in my arms and make love to you again. I may not like what you've said, but I understand. You're afraid of getting hurt once more. Even if I assure you I won't intentionally hurt you, you'll need to find that out for yourself. And to do that, Stacy, the remedy isn't to run away."

"No?"

"No," he said emphatically.

"What's the remedy?" she asked, feeling relieved that the sparring match seemed to be over.

"The remedy," he responded in a very dignified voice, "is to get to know as much about me as possible in the shortest period of time. Then you'll be able to judge for yourself what a really sterling character I am."

Kipp pushed back his chair and stood up. He strode over to the far wall and picked up the phone from its cradle on the built-in desk near the refrigerator. Jokingly, he waved the receiver in her direction. "Unless, of course, you want to save time, and I'll dial Millie for you. She can give you a very biased opinion of my unblemished record." His teasing eased the last vestiges of tension between them.

"Where'd you get such unique remedies, Doctor?" Stacy asked, smiling. The return smile playing across Kipp's face dazzled her. She noticed the cleft in his chin again, the creases fanning away from his eyes, not of anger but of repose.

He focused on a spot over her shoulder. He seemed to be mulling something over. Then his eyes flicked back to her and he said, "How would you like to go out on a date with me? A real honest-to-goodness I'm-glad-I-met-you let's-get-to-know-each-other-better date!"

"No strings attached?" she asked, suddenly wary.

He laughed and the sun seemed to stream a little more brightly through the windows. "Absolutely not," he commented cheerfully. "So, do you think you could handle something as innocuous as that, Stacy?"

"But why?" she asked. "After what I've just told you, why waste your time?"

"Because," he said softly, coming over to stroke

her cheek, "because, I have a vested interest in your well-being."

Her heart beat heavily with joy. "But where does all this leave you?" Looking into his wickedly dancing eyes, she knew she must have turned beet-red.

"Probably taking a lot of cold showers. I'm hoping, of course, our new friendship becomes an old and ripe one fairly soon."

"Why?"

"Guess."

"That's what you said last night, and look where that got me!"

"Us," he answered pointedly, picking up their half-finished mugs of coffee and bringing them over to the sink.

"Now, why don't you go home, change into some beat-up old jeans if you have them, and the three of us will go out on a date. It'll be a shortie because I'm flying to Chicago later today for a medical convention. I'll be gone until Friday night. I was going to tell you before, but we got sidetracked."

"Wait a minute." She threw up her hands. "You're going too fast for me. I haven't even said I'll go. And who's the third party?" she asked with a slight irritation in her voice.

"Connie," he said, as if everyone brought a dog along on a date. "He's a member of this family. In order to know me, you have to know my dog."

"I already know your dog," she said, smiling. "He snores and he has weird eating habits."

"Come on. Don't be a spoil-sport, Stacy. What harm is there in going to the park with Connie and me to play Frisbee? I won't be here all week and he needs his exercise. Besides, a healthy sweat will do you good. Work off some of that excess energy you use for worry."

"Sure, and the only thing I'll get for all my sweat is a shower."

"Yeah," he teased, raising his eyebrows in an old silent-movie-type leer, "but soon we'll be such old friends we can shower together."

"Kipp!" She put on her tough-teacher voice.

"I promise on my oath as a scout to cool it." He wiggled two fingers and she shook her head.

Stacy laughed. Kipp was an overgrown kid. She was partially out the door when she popped her head back in. "You know you're a fraud, don't you?"

He put on a properly offended look. "How can you say such a thing?"

"Because, smartie, if I were going to pretend to be something I'm not, I'd do a little preliminary research."

"And what's that supposed to mean?"

"You're one finger short. A real boy scout holds up three fingers."

"A mere oversight," he quipped to her retreating back.

But when she turned around to playfully stick her tongue out at him, he hastily wiggled a third finger near the other two.

Stacy soon found out that playing Frisbee with Kipp was not easy. Regardless of where she happened to be standing, Kipp invariably looped the disc as far away in the opposite direction as possible. Dressed in scruffy jeans, a Windbreaker with a Mets emblem, and a Yankee baseball hat with the visor at the rear, he assigned Stacy to the Mets and Connie to the Yankees.

"I believe in being ecumenical. It's one of my better traits. You might try remembering that fact."

"Modesty isn't, I notice," she puffed when it was Connie's turn.

Surprisingly, Connie was trained to run only on command. Although his big body shivered mightily with the itch to run, he nevertheless remained by Kipp's side until given his signal.

Stacy's backside took the brunt of the workout. Running sideway and backward in order to keep her eye on the Frisbee, she'd frequently trip and fall into a pile of leaves. When she complained to Kipp, he yelled back at her, "Don't worry, there's plenty of padding there."

So much for compassion and understanding. She swore revenge. With murder in her eye she arced the Frisbee high overhead.

He caught it without moving. "That's not fair." She stamped her feet and swung a fist in his direction. "It's your height and your damned long arms!"

After a fifth throw had her running wildly to the far end of the park's playground, she limped back, panting. "You throw that thing out of bounds all the time. Even Connie gets a fairer shake than I do. This is all a diabolical plot to let the Yankees win!"

"Don't complain," he said, throwing long again. "Connie doesn't need to work off anything stronger than spaghetti and meatballs. You have years of anger to get out of your system."

"Wise guy," she muttered under her breath as she tried to outfly the Frisbee. She caught it and dragged herself back, intent on getting the upper hand.

"Okay, let's see you find this one."

Mustering all her reserve energy, Stacy whipped around, pretending to have thrown the Frisbee. She quickly flopped to the ground and landed on a deep pile of leaves. Then she hurriedly hid the Frisbee behind her back and burrowed into the leaves.

"Connie, fetch!" Kipp shouted.

The dog virtually flew to Stacy, straddled her, pinning her down and thumping his tail in mad abandon.

"Damn your bloodhound nose, Connie!" Stacy's wail turned into a screech when Connie tried to lick her face.

"Good dog," Kipp called triumphantly. He ran over to her to claim his prize.

"That's not fair. You had help."

"Ah-ha!" The light in Kipp's eyes danced with mischief. He pushed Connie away and straddled Stacy himself. "I've finally gotten you right where I want you, fair maiden."

"And where is that, dangerously horrible sir?" she asked.

Kipp's glance slid from her apple-red cheeks to the dried leaves crowning her blond hair. He'd run her ragged and she had never looked more adorable. The worry lines on her forehead were gone. There was no tight expression around her lips. Her eyes sparkled. The teardrops spiking her long lashes were from the sting of the cold November weather. Marshmallow puffs of warm air jetted into the cold as she exhaled. He watched her run her tongue over her dry lips.

Kipp reached down to help her up. The answer to her question was stamped in his eyes. Wordlessly, he gathered her into his arms. He plucked the leaves from the tumble of hair beneath his fingers. She was his wind sprite, and her fragrance combined with the tangy crispness of the autumn cold pulled at his senses. Nestling her in the warm folds of his body, he lowered his lips to hers.

And when he lifted his lips from hers and whispered into her mouth "Look how far we've come already. We've had our first fight and we've weathered the storm. I'm going to miss you, little one. Will you miss me?" her hands crept up to his face. Her fingers lovingly touched the corners of his mouth. Stacy drew his lips back down to hers, answering his question in the best way she knew how.

That night, with Connie snoring softly in the hall outside her room, Stacy lay in her bed missing Kipp. Finally, after listening to the chimes strike two and then three A.M., she slipped out of bed. Careful not to awaken Connie, she went downstairs and removed the cover from her typewriter.

Nine

"Knock, knock, break time. I've brought up some coffee and your manuscript." Pat Lindgren, the school librarian came bustling into the room. Stacy immediately recognized the large manila envelope containing the story she had finished last night when she couldn't sleep thinking about Kipp.

"I hope you're not planning on staying here much longer," Pat added, tilting her head toward the mountain of papers strewn all over Stacy's desk. "It's already way past six."

Stacy dropped her red marking pen. She'd been doodling Kipp's name on a paper instead of finishing her work. Rising, she went to join her spritely colleague.

"How did you know I was dying for a cup of coffee?"

"Because I was. When I noticed your lights on from across the courtyard, I decided to shoo you out. We're both nuts for being here this late. Here," she said. "Let me get your manuscript out of this envelope; I want to talk to you about it."

Stacy tried to hide her anxiety. Pat never pulled

punches when asked for a professional opinion. "I'm almost afraid to ask you if you liked it."

"Let me put your mind at ease right away, Stacy. You've written a winner with this one. I've read it to the third graders, telling the students they were going to hear a story by an unpublished author and that the author wanted their opinions."

"And—?"

"They loved it and so did I," the librarian said, handing Stacy the notes she had jotted of the students' positive opinions.

"Don't be impatient," Pat said, sipping her coffee. "Send this one in to a publisher and keep writing. The characters jump off the page, they're so lifelike. Your drawing of Dr. Jerome Giraffe with that thatch of brown hair falling over an Adidas sweat band really tickled everyone. And all of us thought your adding a dimple in his chin made him especially endearing."

Stacy was thrilled. She couldn't wait for eight o'clock, when Kipp would call from Chicago. He'd phoned Monday and Tuesday evenings and it seemed as if they never ran out of things to say to each other.

"Now, tell me," Pat asked, "where in the world did you dream up the idea for your blue-eyed giraffe hero?"

"Oh," Stacy replied airly, "I patterned him after a physician I know."

"We need more books to lessen young children's fears of going to the hospital."

"That was my aim when I wrote the story," Stacy said, basking in her colleague's endorsement.

"Where on earth did you come up with the idea of a Spanish-speaking marsupial? Did you deliberately choose Manuela because of our large Hispanic population?"

"Actually, I didn't. I took liberties with the gender because I wanted my little kangaroo to have a pouch. Manuela is really a Puerto Rican boy named Manuel who came here for treatment of an obstruction in the terminal ileum which he got as a result of developing adhesions from an appendectomy."

"How do you know about his case so intimately?" Pat asked quickly.

Stacy should have known Pat never missed a trick. She caught the strangely quizzical expression on the librarian's face.

"I learned about Manuel from his physician, the man I patterned the giraffe after. He's also my neighbor. When my foot was hurt, he helped me. Manuel sent me a Spanish-language comic book to keep me company."

"And this doctor also spoke to Manuel about you? Isn't that unusual?"

"Perhaps, but Dr. Palmer knows I'm a teacher. Manuel was here alone. His parents were too poor to remain with him the whole time he was hospitalized. I just gave Kipp some advice about boys Manuel's age, that's all."

"So this Kipp in real life is your doctor, too, besides being your neighbor?"

"Yes."

"I see. . . ." Pat's thoughtful expression brightened with an idea. "If Dr. Palmer is anything like the warm, generous character you drew in your story, he must be a very special person. Career Day's coming up. Why not invite your doctor to come and speak to the students?"

Stacy smiled, feeling a rush of warmth. *My doctor.* The words had a nice ring to them. Yes, she thought, why not invite Kipp for Career Day? She couldn't wait to see the other women's reaction to him. If any of them got too chummy, she'd put a "Taken" sign on him.

"What'll you give me if I say yes?" Kipp's deep voice lowered an octave and Stacy heard his heavy breathing heating up the phone lines from Chicago.

"You make a lousy masher," she said, stifling her giggles.

"Don't change the subject."

"That's blackmail and you know it."

"Right," Kipp agreed wholeheartedly.

They'd been speaking for fifteen minutes and she'd finally gotten around to mentioning Career Day. Who could blame him for sounding less than enthusiastic? The idea of facing her feisty group of independent souls could be terrifying for a grown-up. She couldn't wait to see his reaction to them.

"A doctor's time is valuable," she said sympathetically, getting ready for the kill.

"You bet it is." He chuckled and she wished she could kiss him right then, hard. "So you'd better make it worth my while."

"What d'ya all want, honey?" she drawled.

"For openers, I want to chase you around your classroom with all the kids screaming 'dirty old man' or 'masher' or whatever kids scream nowadays. Then I want to catch you, grab your cute little derriere, and smooch. I've always had this thing about chasing a pretty teacher around the room."

"Kipp! Watch what you're saying, honeychile. The operator might be listening."

"Good," he said. "Let's talk dirty and give the operator some really hot ideas."

"You're incorrigible."

"Wrong. I'm missing you. I want to play with you,

good, healthy adult games. I want to roll around on a bed with you, none of this kid stuff where we only hold hands. What I want is some heavy petting, and, you're right, I'd better shut up. I'm not doing my blood pressure any good." A distinctly male growling sound burned the line.

"That's what I said. You're incorrigible." Stacy lay on the bed, her face wreathed in smiles. She wanted to tell him in person how much he meant to her. She loved him, loved his caring ways, loved his patience with her, loved him for all the qualities she missed in a partner. In no time he'd wangled his way into her affections, and now he was stuck there for good. Three days without seeing him was driving her up the wall.

She twirled the phone cord around her little finger, imagining she was twirling his hair instead. Propped against two pillows, her feet beat time to the soft rock music on the radio. Connie was stretched out on the floor beside the bed, his eyes and nose twitching as he dreamed.

"Will you settle for a good home-cooked meal when you come home Friday night?" she asked, and immediately wondered what lunacy prompted her to issue the invitation. She couldn't cook!

"Is that your best offer?"

"For the present," Stacy answered, getting a grip on her heartbeat. Her blood pressure wasn't 120 over 80 either.

"Can you cook?" Kipp demanded.

"Of course I can cook." Stacy heard the croak in her voice and hoped Kipp thought it was static on the line. The only thing she had in common with Julia Child was dropping food! Cooking simply didn't interest her.

After two months of Stacy's cooking, Harry had

practically begged to be chef. She knew all about good nutrition. And she knew which minerals and vitamins went with what food group. She'd even chastised Kipp about his eating habits, but knowing about a subject and applying that knowledge over a hot stove were too distinctly different things!

When she did cook, her main dishes consisted of fifty ways to prepare canned water-packed tuna fish. She'd never yet unmolded her sugarless Jell-O when it hadn't flattened like the old college razz for the losing team. On the rare occasions she'd tried her hand at making fruit pies, the pie crust burned on cue, and everyone except herself thought she made the worst coffee in the world. Even her own parents had pronounced it mud.

"My culinary arts are well known." She crossed two fingers and tried to think of a way to feed Kipp the dinner she'd promised. She was running low on ingenuity.

"In fact," she added, slowly sinking deeper into her own quicksand, "I once turned down an offer to attend the Culinary Institute in Hyde Park."

That part was true. Her parents wanted her to let them pay for the course. To help find the next husband, they intimated. When she refused, they'd bought her a microwave oven to heat TV dinners.

"In that case," Kipp said, accepting the offer, "I can't wait to taste your cooking. I've always said the way to a man's heart is through his stomach, especially when you've rejected the more direct route."

"So, may I count on you for Career Day?" She might as well salvage something out of this. By Friday night, unless she came up with a miracle, the pot would be boiling and she'd be the main course!

"All right. Have someone at your school call my secretary and set up the schedule. And Stacy . . . ?"

"Yes?"

"I . . . uh . . . never mind, I'll tell you Friday. By the way, what were you doing when I called?"

Waiting by the phone. Counting the minutes. Watching the digital clock numbers move. Reading a book upside down. Thinking about you and the way you make me feel. Thinking that I love you. Thinking what a fool I've been and how we've wasted time. Take your pick.

"Nothing special," she said, plucking an idea from her fertile store of unused pranks. "I was doing a crossword puzzle, but I'm stuck on a word. It's on the tip of my tongue too."

"Maybe I can help? After all, I don't want you to go to bed as frustrated as I am."

"Take two aspirin and call me in the morning," she quipped.

"Very funny," he said sourly. "Aspirin won't help my problem."

"Then take a cold shower," she said sweetly. If she could take them, so could he! "You offered to help me with my missing word. So here goes. He's tall and graceful. It's a popular, stately, long-necked animal that has brown spots and sexy blue eyes!"

"That's easy, but the eyes are brown, not blue. It's a giraffe. I always liked those animals. And you're right. There is something sexy about them."

"You're so right," she whispered huskily, failing to hide the bubble of laughter in her voice.

"Stacy . . . ?"

"Mmm?"

"Don't make dessert. I've got my own ideas about that."

"Good night, Kipp," she said. "I can't wait to taste your mystery dessert."

Many sleepless hours later Stacy vowed to find a

culture that believed in serving the dessert course before the main meal. It was her only salvation.

Kipp rolled over on the bed and pushed the phone off his stomach. He was sweating. Stacy's purred good night could light any man's fire. He'd come that close to blurting out that he loved her, but thank goodness he'd checked himself in time. No way was he going to scare her off again and risk ending his second chance with her.

He tried to sort out the difference in Stacy tonight. He'd sensed a difference the minute she started talking. Her guard was down. In its place the real Stacy emerged, playful and warm, the way he remembered her the night they'd made love.

Maybe absence did make the heart grow fonder. It sure did where he was concerned. Tonight she was like an excited kid, and he couldn't wait to get home to her. She'd told him she'd written another story. When he pressed her for details, she'd clammed up, claiming it was bad luck. If that were the case, he thought, why had she told him all about the story she'd sent to *Humpty Dumpty* magazine?

That was part of it. All he had to do was make the connection. He racked his brain for the answer. What had she said? Sexy blue eyes? On a giraffe? Whom was she kidding? Crossword puzzle, his foot!

In a flash of cognition he made a beeline for the phone. As he placed his unique request with F.A.O. Schwarz, he wished he could be a fly on the wall and watch Stacy's face when she saw her surprise.

The United Parcel delivery truck was parked outside Stacy's home just as she pulled into the driveway the following day. Scooting out of her car, she reached her front door in time to see a burly delivery man filling out a Sorry We Missed You form. Between the man's bulk and her door stood a long rectangular box.

"May I help you?" she inquired politely.

"Are you Stacy Conklin?" The scribbling halted. His pencil remained poised on the pad.

"Yes, but you probably have the wrong house. I didn't order anything."

"Lady, this thing is heavy. Besides, it's pretty near six feet tall and if your name is Conklin, it's yours."

The fancily wrapped gift box came from F.A.O. Schwarz on Fifth Avenue in New York. "There has to be some mistake," she insisted.

"Mrs. Conklin, do you mind checking the contents? Maybe it'll jar your mind, or maybe your husband bought you a present?" He tapped on his watch. "I'd hate to have to come back here tomorrow."

"All right. But you'll only have to pack whatever is in there up again and lug it right back to the truck."

Two minutes later she clapped her hands and let out a screech. Then she started laughing as she looked up toward the ceiling. "Oh, Kipp," she murmured, falling in love with the stuffed animal. "Only you would find a blue-eyed six-foot giraffe."

The delivery man looked greatly relieved. Connie heard all the commotion and clunked down the stairs to sniff at the new arrival. A dual-resident dog, he'd moved in with Stacy during Kipp's absence.

"I take it you're prepared to keep this thing," the UPS man commented wryly, drawing her attention away from Kipp's present.

"Keep it?" She stared at the delivery man as if

he'd taken leave of his senses for implying otherwise. "I'd kill for it. That's Dr. Jerome Giraffe."

Stacy hastened to press a generous tip in the man's palm. With a quick kiss on the giraffe's rump, she ran to her purse to examine the balance in her checking account.

Telling her conscience it was for a good cause, she dialed the Goose and Gander restaurant to plan her home-cooked meal with Chef Louis Bertrand.

Then she phoned Bev to check up on the progress of her pregnancy. When she heard her friend was spotting, she worriedly cautioned her to rest a lot.

"Stop sounding like Vito. I've spotted before and I'm taking it easy. After all, I'm going to be a bride soon," she said, reminding Stacy of the annual hospital fund-raiser at the country club. "Now, tell me what's happening with you?"

Stacy filled her in on the latest news. When she got to the part about inviting Kipp for a home-cooked meal, Bev exploded in laughter.

"You'd be better off if you just dragged him to a restaurant and footed the bill," Bev said.

"Great minds run in the same direction, smartie."

"You mean you're actually going to take Kipp to a restaurant after all that hype about your culinary skills?"

"No, silly," Stacy replied, her plans all set, "I'm going to buy American."

"What's that supposed to mean?"

"That I believe in spreading the wealth. Tomorrow, when Kipp comes over, he's going to have a veritable banquet of gastronomic delights courtesy of the Goose and Gander."

"You're kidding, aren't you? That's one of the most expensive restaurants around here."

"No, I'm not kidding, and stop exciting yourself.

It's no good for what's-his-name. Any man who springs for a blue-eyed giraffe deserves the best. That's the Goose and Gander restaurant. To keep it technically honest, the dinner will be served in my house. We're have galantine of goose filled with veal mousse and pistachios served with a sauce of peach brandy, wild mushrooms and goose stock, plus an endive and radicchio salad accompanied by a raspberry-walnut dressing."

"What? No appetizer?"

"Don't be catty. I thought I'd do that part myself. I do have some talents."

"I'm impressed. Poor Kipp," Bev said, laughing.

"So am I, Bev. Believe me, poor Kipp will be divinely happy before the night is out."

Stacy pictured the intimate evening, replete with sterling silver candlesticks, her best Irish linen tablecloth, her finest Mikasa service, and her, looking glamorous in a black chiffon wraparound dress with its plunging neckline, not a hair out of place as she romantically served the meal to end all meals. If she played her cards right, Kipp wouldn't know what to taste first.

"It isn't every day I can sit in the beauty parlor while cooking a four-star meal at the same time, is it?"

Ten

Stacy congratulated herself on how well her split-second timing was going. Absolutely nothing was going to go wrong tonight as long as she had anything to say about it. Proper planning and preparation was nine tenths of winning. That's what her father always drummed into her head. *Tonight, Dad,* she thought smugly, *you'd be proud of me!*

After school she'd driven straight to the beauty parlor to have her hair styled. "I want the wild and windblown look," she announced as she gratefully accepted a cup of coffee from Sadie, her hairdresser.

"In other words," Sadie said, looking at her in the mirror, "you wanna look sexy. Hey, don't blush. It's okay. If I had your looks, I'd use 'em too."

Stacy had no time to blush. "Right," she agreed. "Sexy, but in control. Can you do that?"

Sadie's talented hands could do just that and did.

She'd arrived home just as the food was being delivered from the Goose and Gander. "Any special instructions from Chef Bertrand?" she asked the delivery man as she opened the door to let him pass.

"Not that I know of. The chef told me he's already spoken to someone about that. I assume that's you."

"I don't remember. He probably did say something when I ordered the food, but it slipped my mind. Anyway, there's no problem. You're here with the order, which was my biggest worry. All the rest is smooth sailing." She handed him a check and a tip.

She had a half hour to put the goose into the oven on a low temperature, to light the candles and the log in the fireplace in the dining room, and to change into her evening attire. She'd dashed home during lunch and taken a quick shower. Thank goodness, she thought, her school was only three miles away.

Her black chiffon wrap dress, her lingerie, including garter belt, the dramatic sheer black hosiery with the lacy design, her sling-back pumps, her cosmetics, and her perfume were waiting in the downstairs powder room. With good luck there'd be no reason to go upstairs.

As she slipped into the dramatically sexy dress and secured the rhinestone clip at the waist, she felt in total control of her life for the first time in a long time. The only thing that could have marred her plans was an unexpected snowfall preventing Kipp from flying home from Chicago, and that hadn't happened.

When the doorbell rang, she flew to answer it on the first ring. Kipp, arms laden with yellow roses and a bottle of wine, let out a long, low wolf whistle as soon as he saw Stacy.

"You like?" she asked, pirouetting quickly for his inspection.

"I more than like," he said with an adulatory grin as she practically yanked him across the threshold and into the dimly lit hallway.

" 'Scuse my rush." She flung herself into his open

arms. "This is for the giraffe"—Stacy nibbled her way up Kipp's neck to torment his earlobe—"and this is for me." Her voice was husky when she spoke and her eyes were filled with happiness.

She had imagined this moment all day. Now that it was here and she could feel the heat emanating from his body, she wanted to bury herself in his warmth. Her arms looped around his waist, hugging him tightly to her.

"More, please," she demanded, struggling not to devour him while he put down his packages.

"If this is what I have to look forward to when I come home, I'm going to go away more often."

"I've got the schedule all made out. It's for short trips with lots of hellos and good-byes. We'll be teary-eyed for the good-byes. Now kiss me with pizzazz, please."

"Like this?" he whispered, breathing the words into her mouth as he obligingly fit his lips to hers.

She squeezed her eyes shut, letting Kipp work his magic. Her nails dug into the jacket of his suit to feel the hard musculature beneath the surface. She floated in the trancelike sensations of his kiss. Again and again he kissed her and rubbed his hands on her derriere while her hands restlessly moved to clutch his head. He rocked his lips back and forth until she felt her insides go soft and moist.

"You look gorgeous," she said when they finally surfaced for air. "You smell gorgeous too."

"You too. What's the name of that perfume?"

"Seduction. What else?" she said, batting her eyelashes.

"Stacy, I missed you." He tilted her face up to his. "There's a freedom about you now. I sensed it when we spoke on the phone. Care to tell me what I owe my good fortune to?"

"Don't look a gift horse in the mouth." She melted back into his arms and mewed contentedly. "You're doing just fine."

His eyes were dancing wickedly. His mouth bent in a smile. With her help he shrugged out of his suit jacket.

"Anything to please a lady," he said obligingly.

Then he dipped his head to hers to capture her lips in another soul-drenching kiss. His hand was gliding up and down the outside of her dress, and she invitingly guided it beneath the hem of the black chiffon froth. Lifting the tissue-thin layers of the flimsy material, his fingers stroked the soft skin of her thigh. She knew she'd set him up like a shameless hussy. She giggled as the hand gliding upward caressed a sensuously bare buttock.

A bare buttock!

He peeled his lips from hers. He pulled only slightly away. His eyes widened in pleasurable surprise. Her chuckle wafted up to him.

"You vamp! You're not wearing underpants!"

His hand whipped out from beneath the dress to rush to her bosom. Slipping his fingers into the deeply plunging neckline, he took the weight of a bare breast in his hand and kneaded the soft mound.

"What are you trying to do to me?" He groaned, crushing her hips against his hard arousal.

She pulled away. Playing the wanton temptress, she unhooked the rhinestone clip at her waistline. The dress fell to the floor in a cloud of triumph. "I really can't have you chasing me around my classroom on Career Day," she murmured huskily. "So I thought I'd let you live out your fantasies now."

"Here? Now?" His eyebrows shot up in surprise.

"It's your fantasy," she said, mesmerized by the wolfish gleam in his eye. She tugged at his zipper.

"What about dinner? Won't it spoil?" he asked.

"Ah, you silly man. Don't you know this is the appetizer?"

Completely relaxed in the afterglow of their frenzied lovemaking, Kipp strolled into the dining room. He and Stacy had used the downstairs powder room to freshen up. Now, he'd noted with some satisfaction, she had first aid supplies in the medicine cabinet. It was amazing how so much had happened between the two of them since he'd cleaned and bandaged her foot. He sent a silent thank-you to his now well-oiled garage door track.

A fire had been lit in the dining room's fireplace, giving it a cozy, intimate feeling. He stretched his arms out on the mantel and gazed into the embers as he thought about Stacy. She was an outrageous tease, a sly minx, and a delightful combination of surprises, and he loved her all the more because of it. He still couldn't believe she'd seduced him in the hallway, of all places. Thank goodness there was an inner door from the front porch and no one could see them.

That Stacy no longer wore her wedding band was another positive sign of her freedom from the shackles of her past marriage. He'd never asked her about the reasons she'd still kept it on. Privately, he'd hated it. Every time he saw the ring it reminded him of a golden yoke, a symbol to him of the limitations she placed on men in her life. Encouraged by her new, carefree attitude, his hopes rose. But would she want to replace Harry's ring with his? The question daunted him for days. Still, he knew better than to press her. For now he'd be content to let her set their romantic pace.

Humming happily, Stacy heard Kipp calling to her from the other room. "I think we've earned a drink. What'll you have?"

"How about some of the wine you brought?" She surveyed the domestic scene in the kitchen and concluded she enjoyed the role. It was a brand new experience for her, wanting to become a fine cook like Chef Bertrand and prepare fancy dishes for Kipp. She decorated the galantine of goose with a garnish of watercress and maraschino cherries and carried the platter into the dining room to join him.

"There," she said, carefully setting down the platter near his plate so he could do the honors, "doesn't this look nice?"

"It sure does."

Was Kipp a ventriloquist?

She was certain his lips hadn't moved. Yet, that was definitely a man's voice she heard.

A male voice!

It couldn't be? Could it?

Her stomach reached her knees as she grabbed for the back of a chair. For an instant her eyes locked with Kipp's in disbelief. He was looking at her strangely, as if she'd miraculously become a baritone. He'd heard it too.

They weren't alone!

Someone else was in the house!

Sheer panic ripped through Stacy's body as she recognized the marvelously dashing figure of the man entering the room.

Dressed in a three-piece blue suit, and more devastatingly handsome than she remembered, her exhusband strolled over to her, acting as if he'd never been away.

He was as good-looking as ever: athletically trim, tall, with calm green eyes, thick eyelashes, sensuous lips, and a perfect, even tan that emphasized the whiteness of his teeth.

"Harry!" she screamed, finally finding her voice. "What are you doing here?"

"What the . . . !" Kipp's eyes veered from Stacy to Harry.

"Hello, babe." Harry put his arms on Stacy's shoulders. "As usual, you look like a vision. I hope you don't mind. When I got in, you weren't home, so I went upstairs to our bedroom to catch some shuteye. It's been a long trip. I'll tell you all about it later."

"Your bedroom? What the hell is going on here?" Kipp bellowed in exasperation. "How did you get in here without a key?"

"Oh, but I have my key, don't I, babe?" Harry waved the key under Kipp's nose like a red cape in a bullfight. "See."

"Give me that!" Stacy grabbed the key from Harry's hand. She immediately regretted not changing all the locks on the door the minute he'd left.

Glaring suspiciously at Stacy, Kipp threw his hands up.

Stacy stared at the unreal tableau. It took her several seconds to absorb the Kafkaesque scene unfolding before her eyes. She knew her own face must be a duplicate of the ashen pallor on Kipp's. Her ex-husband, her lover, and her! Under one roof!

Oh, my God! After she and Kipp just got through . . . !

It couldn't be! Harry had to be a figment of her imagination. But figments don't walk, they don't smile, and they certainly don't bend down to kiss your cheek!

Disbelievingly, she looked first at one and then the other man. She simply couldn't function rationally.

"Good Lord!" Kipp cried.

She didn't have to guess what he was thinking about. His rage was unmistakable. Whatever the story behind Harry's sudden reappearance, she and Kipp could have been caught in the most compromising position.

She began to shake as though she'd been caught in violent air turbulence. She fought to get her mouth to work, to push down the gorge rising in her throat. How much had Harry seen and heard?

As if in answer to her unspoken question, Harry repeated, "I've been napping in our bedroom."

"That's not our bedroom!"

"Sure it is," he said cheerfully. "Since when do you go in for stuffed giraffes, babe?"

"I don't believe this," Kipp said, and Harry turned to him.

In a nightmarish haze Stacy watched her former husband charmingly extend his hand to Kipp in greeting. Acting as if they'd both invited him for dinner, Harry said, "We haven't been formally introduced. I'm Harry Conklin." When Kipp's mouth stayed shut, Stacy weakly supplied his name.

The shock had reached her arteries, immobilizing her. Harry took both of her hands in his and she simply stared at them in his grasp.

"When did you learn how to cook, babe?"

Tomorrow she'd wake up and find out she'd come in in the middle of a bad dream. Was it possible that Harry was talking to her as though this weren't the first conversation he'd had with her in almost a year?

"If I remember correctly," Harry was announcing pleasantly, "I did all the cooking in the four years we were married. Honey, the dining room looks marvelous. You always did set a beautiful table. I must say ordering from the Goose and Gander was a stroke of genius. Chef Bertrand called before. I'm sorry I fell asleep, or I would have helped you prepare for your dinner party. You know"—he winked, patting her on the top of her head to a stunned Kipp—"one of these days you'll learn how to cook, won't you, babe?"

The dinner! Harry let the cat out of the bag and told Kipp she couldn't cook! With any luck the floor would open up and she'd disappear. Stacy braced herself for the worst. She knew why this was happening to her. She was being paid back for all her crazy tricks! Some power higher than she was seeing to it she got her just deserts!

Chancing a glance at Kipp, she saw the devilish glint in his eyes. She almost dropped dead when she heard him say to Harry, "Oh, I don't think she's such a bad cook. She makes a great appetizer."

"Really." Harry glanced at her with new respect. "I'd like to try it."

"No." Stacy choked and began to cough.

"Harry, bring her some water," Kipp demanded brusquely, neatly eliminating Harry from the room.

Kipp didn't fool her one bit. Underneath his bantering Stacy knew he was as close as she'd ever seen him to blowing up. A scant second later she found out how right she was.

"Do you realize how close we came to being caught? How do we find out if he saw us?" Kipp hissed the moment they were alone.

She hadn't planned this and she wasn't going to take the blame. "You certainly don't expect me to ask him as the party of the third part if he'd seen the party of the first part diddling the party of the second part do you?" she hissed back, thoroughly upset.

"Why aren't you angrier at seeing him?" Kipp fumed, keeping her blood pressure up.

"How do you know how I feel?" She bristled at the insinuation. "In case you don't know it, I'm just as flabbergasted as you are, buster."

"Let's not argue the point, dammit. Is his catatonic double still upstairs?"

"What's that got to do with the price of tea in China? For your information, it's upstairs in the closet. It's too unwieldy for me to put in the garbage."

Kipp banged his fist on the table and rattled the stemware. "I wish I had the right to throw both of them the hell out."

"They why don't you?" she said, clutching at straws.

"Because this is your house and so far I can't see any evidence that he's trying to harm you."

"Then what's he trying to do?"

"Get back into your pants, to put it crudely, you little naïve schoolteacher."

Before she could fire off a protest that she wasn't a naive schoolteacher, the kitchen door swung open and Harry breezed back into the room. Switching to a headwaiter routine, he solicitously handed her a glass of water.

"Listen, I don't want to be a party pooper. Why don't you two go ahead and eat? I'm not hungry. Tell you what, I'll even serve you." He pulled the chairs out and motioned them to sit down.

"This food's too expensive to waste, isn't it, babe?" He turned and left them staring at his back as he went through the swinging doors to the kitchen.

Kipp was livid. "If he calls you babe one more time, I'm going to shove my fist in his face. Does that nut really expect me to eat this meal? A meal which you didn't cook, incidentally."

"Good intentions count for something, don't they?" she asked, trying to soothe his feelings.

Kipp never had a chance to reply. Harry came in balancing a plate of salad on each palm.

"Ah-ha, here we are. Just like old times, isn't it, babe? You remember our dinner parties. All the fun we had. Oh, say, Kipp, I didn't mean to shut you out with our reminiscences. Forgive me." He set the endive and radicchio salads in front of them. Then he began to spoon on the raspberry-walnut dressing. "The salads look delicious," he said as he stepped back to admire the table. "Dig in, folks."

Stacy automatically lifted her fork. It clattered back onto her plate as she caught the murderous look on Kipp's face.

"It needs rolls." Harry said, hovering over Stacy and Kipp. "I could whip them up in ten minutes. Do you want rolls?"

"No!" Stacy screeched.

"Sure, Harry." Kipp said between clenched teeth. "Go whip up some rolls."

Harry smiled benevolently at both of them. "Be back in a jiffy. Now, don't say anything interesting until I get back."

"I can't believe you!" Kipp charged as they heard Harry whistling in the kitchen.

"Me!" Stacy exploded. "What did I do?"

"How can you be so foolish as to not change the locks on your doors?"

"Because I never expected to be served dinner by my ex-husband while my date and I sat down to a meal in my house."

"And Millie thought life in the suburbs might be too dull for me!"

"I didn't plan this," Stacy said, spitting out her fury. "Harry did."

"So what are you going to do about it?"

"Find out why he's here. I know he wants something," she fired back.

"That's obvious, you little fool. I already told you what he wants. He wants you. Whatever happened to what's-her-name? The one he dumped you for?"

"That's a cheap shot and you know it. Her name's Mona. What's the name of the man you caught Felicia with?"

Kipp expelled a heavy breath. He rubbed his forehead. He spread his hands out in an open gesture and picked up her hand before he said quietly, "You know he's got us fighting, don't you?"

Nodding, she sat in misery, buried in her glum thoughts. It was true. Harry had tornadoed himself back, leaving a destructive path. Even the twinkling candles seemed to mock her. The intimate dinner for two had become a shambles, and her ex-husband was in the kitchen making rolls!

Why not? She was in a lunatic asylum and she was the head lunatic!

"Here we are." Harry pivoted back into the room with a basket of hot rolls. "You understand, don't you, old chap. We haven't seen each other in a long time." He pulled a chair out and sat down next to Stacy. "We have a lot to catch up on."

"We're divorced, Harry."

"I know, babe, but we can remedy that. Go ahead," he said, waving at the food on the table, "eat. I'll just pick."

Stacy was too shocked to reply. She'd fantasized conversations with Harry over the past long months where she'd tell him off in no uncertain terms. Now, in front of Kipp, he was actually telling her he wanted her back.

Kipp leaned back in the chair. He folded his arms

across his chest. "So tell us, Harry, old chap, where've you been all this time while you left Stacy to fend for herself?"

"Ah. Touché. I dare-say the answer to that might take hours, but it's all quite explainable. Try some more of the raspberry-walnut dressing. It's quite good."

Stacy had enough. "I don't want any raspberry-walnut dressing. Answer Kipp's question, Harry. I'd heard through the grapevine you and Mona were on a yacht somewhere in the Caribbean. What happened? Did it sink in shallow waters and everyone on board was lost but you?"

"Hardly. You know no one ever understood me the way you did, babe."

"Translated, she dumped you. Isn't that right, Harry?"

"Even I'm interested in that answer, old chap," Kipp said, viewing Harry with the first hint of a smile Stacy had seen since this farce had begun.

"A gentleman doesn't answer a question like that."

Score one for charming Harry, Stacy thought. He'd wiggled out of another answer.

Stacy glanced at Kipp and saw the calm determination in his face, but she was surprised when he rose and said, "I'd better go and let you two talk this out."

"See here, Kipp, I didn't mean to break up this little dinner party. You don't have to run off just yet, do you?"

"I make it a practice not to include men on my dates. Stacy and I will have plenty of time, I assure you."

"But we've hardly had a chance to talk," Harry said gallantly. "What about all this goose?"

"You eat the goose, Harry. I think it's cooked just right for you."

"Kipp, don't go."

"It's all right, babe." Kipp winked at her surprised look. "Stacy, walk with me into the hall, will you?"

As Kipp slipped into his coat, she tugged at his arm. "This is crazy. Why are you leaving? Harry's the one who should leave, not you."

"Three's a crowd. I've been watching your reaction to him. Talk to him. Clear the air once and for all. Be certain of your feelings. I'm gambling you'll be the better off for it. After he's gone there's something I want to ask you." He held her to him in a swift embrace.

"But I love you, you nut," she cried in desperation. "Don't go. You don't know Harry. He's as smooth as an eel. He goaded you and you fell for it."

Kipp leaned over and kissed her, brushing her gently with his mouth. He took her hand from his sleeve and gave her a pat on her backside.

"You're throwing me to the wolves because you're pissed off," she wailed miserably.

"No, I'm not. It's just time for you to test your reaction to Chef Boyardee in there."

"I don't take tests. I give them. If you leave now, it's because you're chicken." She should have let Kipp punch Harry when she had the chance.

"I'm not chicken," Kipp said, and she heard the impatient note creep into his voice. "Believe me, this is one of my more daring acts."

"I think Ed Stein would say you're a fool."

"Perhaps. Send me a signal when the coast is clear and I'll come back."

"What kind of a signal?" she sniffed, clutching at his jacket.

"I'll be in my bedroom. You can play Paul Revere

with the shade. You know. One pull if you need help, two when the coast is clear."

"Why can't I just phone?" Her voice was shaky. She was miserable. This was not the evening she'd planned.

"Where's your sense of adventure?" he quipped as he closed the front door behind him.

He hadn't heard her when she told him she loved him. *Harry, you no good louse, why couldn't you have stayed away for good?*

Stacy walked with a heavy heart back into the dining room. She wasn't looking forward to the confrontation with Harry.

"All right, Harry," she said, "we're alone. There's no grandstand for you to play to. You waltz back into my house, *my* house, Harry, not yours, and you try to throw my life into chaos. Why?"

"I know I deserve this, babe . . ."

"Harry, watch my lips. If you call me babe one more time, I'm going to go in the kitchen, grab a frying pan, and bop you over the head with it. Cut it out. You never called me babe before, so don't start now. What are you doing here anyway?"

"I told you, I missed you."

"Baloney. Where are you working, Harry?"

"What's that got to do with it?"

"Call it curiosity?"

"I'm starting a job in South Jersey soon. It's in computer sales. You know, that's the field of today and tomorrow, not like some of these other industries that are falling on hard times."

Stacy didn't want to go into a discussion of the many mergers in the computer industry. She'd been through so many false starts with Harry.

"Mona threw you out, didn't she?"

"We decided to end it a long time ago. Her husband dangled some diamonds in her face and her eyes lit up."

"So we come to the truth at last."

The silence spread between them. "You're in love with him, aren't you?" he said finally, and she heard the desperation in his voice.

"That's none of your business, Harry. Neither one of us has a claim on the other."

"Are you going to marry him?"

She found herself answering him anyway. "I don't know. We haven't talked about that. I'm not sure what I want. You did a pretty good number on me in that department."

"I'm sorry. How's your writing?"

They were alone with no audience for him to perform to. Stacy shrugged her shoulders and sat down again. They could have been two distant cousins catching up on old family news. She'd thought about this meeting many times, first wondering if it would ever come to be, and then wondering how she'd handle it. She'd even fantasized their conversation. In them she always raked him over the coals, getting the satisfaction she'd never been able to have in person.

Her opportunity was now. He'd sought her out. He wanted her again, not the other way around. She looked at him carefully. He seemed strained, not his usual patronizing self. He was grasping at straws and she knew it.

"Same as always," she said in answer to his question about her writing. "Except I'm getting better. One of these days I might even be published. Of course, I'm still writing children's stories. You always said there was no money in that, didn't you?"

"I was wrong."

"You were wrong about a lot of things."

Where was the personal thrill she'd expected? Why wasn't she dishing out the acerbic comments she'd practiced? She didn't feel anger. Instead, she recognized another emotion: pity. He was still handsome. He'd still go on breaking hearts and living by his wits and charm if he could. But now, sitting across from her, she saw something else. The act he'd put on for Kipp had drained him. His confidence was gone. His shoulders sagged. She noticed for the first time the frayed collar on his shirt.

"Harry," she said wearily as she rose to close the conversation, "you'd better go."

His hand touched hers, staying her from seeing him out. His eyes beseeched hers. "Stacy, it's late. Would you mind if I slept over? I'll take the couch."

Now she understood the real reason he'd come back into her life. Piecing together the little he'd told her, she realized he was down on his luck again. She'd been so worried about herself for so long, she hadn't realized just how lucky she was. She felt loved and was ready to pour that love out on Kipp.

The anger she'd been carrying around with her all these months slid from her body in a rush. This man sitting near her was an adolescent frozen in a time warp she'd gladly left.

She thought of Kipp—Kipp, whose looks could never equal Harry's, but whose heart blazed with beauty. He'd wanted her to confront her demons, and she did, once and for all. How wise of him. She compared Kipp's lack of vanity to Harry's usual over-abundance, and she knew that Harry, like the proverbial bad penny, would bounce back again. She thought of all the times Kipp had bolstered her flagging spirits. She considered Harry's request and knew she couldn't let him stay.

He'd caused her so much heartache and aggravation, yet in a way she owed him a debt. He'd given her back the rest of her life. She'd learned a lot because of Harry. She'd become resilient and independent. She now had the confidence in herself to keep trying her hand at writing, but most of all she was free to love again.

"Harry," she said gently, "wait here. I'll be right down."

She went upstairs, leaving Harry alone in the room. She wanted to end the painful encounter as soon as possible.

In her brightly lit room she went straight to the night table by the bed. She opened a drawer and reached in the back for an envelope.

"What are you doing, Stacy?" Harry stood in the doorway quietly watching her. "That's where you keep your mad money, isn't it?"

"Yes." She smiled sadly, her eyes shimmering with tears. He'd always be a little lost boy to her. "I thought you could use this for a motel room, Harry. I don't think it's wise for you to stay."

He walked over to where she was standing in front of the drawn window shade. "You're all grown-up, aren't you, Stacy?"

Nodding, the tears coursed unchecked down her cheeks. There were tears in the handsome face smiling down at her. He had been her sun god for so long. Her bottom lip trembled as she struggled to retain her composure.

"Let's make a pact not to hurt each other anymore—okay, Harry?"

He hesitated for the briefest of seconds. He said softly, "I should have kept you when I had the chance.

You always were the rainbow, only I never knew it."
Leaning forward, he touched her forehead with his.
"Be happy, Stacy."

"You too, Harry, you too."

"One last embrace for old time's sake, Stacy. I
never meant to hurt you."

"I know." Her breath caught on a sob. He opened
his arms and she hugged him the way she'd have
hugged one of her students.

He took her face in his palms. "Not like that,
Stacy."

She felt his lips claim hers. For a brief moment
she struggled, then stopped. It was such a little
thing for her to do. In her heart she knew she was
saying good-bye. It was time to write *finis* to a painful chapter in her life.

She switched off the light and walked down the
stairs with Harry to see him to the door. Kipp was
right. He had waited for her to be free of the past.
That's why he hadn't answered her when she told
him she loved him. She'd learned that to be free to
love, truly love, she needed to put the pain behind
her, and she'd done that at last.

She rushed back upstairs to change her clothes
and signal to Kipp the coast was clear.

Kipp cursed himself for a fool. He'd gambled all
right. He'd gambled and lost! She'd told him she
loved him and then turned around and deceived
him. He'd seen their silhouettes behind the shade in
the bedroom window. Stacy and Harry. Together,
holding each other and kissing. Oh, he'd gotten the
signal all right. This time Harry wasn't the dummy.
He was. And he wasn't going to wait around for more

punishment. Nor did he ever want to speak to Stacy again.

He felt as if he'd aged a hundred years. He sat down at his desk to look for the address of the realtor who'd rented the house to him. Tomorrow he'd instruct her to break the lease regardless of cost.

He programmed his phone to forward all calls to his office, where his secretary would be given strict instructions to tell Stacy he was out. He'd also have her phone Stacy's school to inform them his schedule wouldn't permit his attending Career Day. It would save them both needless embarrassment. Calling for Connie to go with him, Kipp threw some clothes into his car and rapidly sped away. He couldn't spend another night in that house.

Stacy was right about one thing.

Ed Stein would call him a fool.

Eleven

"Millie, don't bug me. Just let me be. I've been through this before and I've lived. Believe me, with all my experience, I'm growing the hide of a rhinoceros."

Kipp stiffened as his sister put her hand on his shoulder. Moving out of her reach, he paced the living room between the couch and the window. He'd been prowling their house at night for the last three weeks, probably keeping Frank and her up too. Sleep was no friend to him. Whenever he closed his eyes, he pictured Stacy in Harry's arms returning his kiss. In the back of his mind he'd been afraid of what might have happened after he left them alone, but it was a chance he convinced himself he needed to take before he made a complete fool of himself.

Whatever passed between Stacy and him was an interlude, the kind that happened between grown people all the time, he thought. No promises were made. She owed him nothing. So why did he feel as if there were an empty void where his heart should be?

"You know what, little brother?"

"Don't throw your three-minute head start up to me." Kipp tried to help ease the tension. "I told you I'll be all right. I've planned some trips. It's time I took a vacation anyway."

Kipp steeled himself to erase his vivid memory of the torrid love scene with Stacy when she seduced him in her hallway. He winced as he remembered her satiny voice teasing him, telling him she'd planned short trips for him so they could relive the fun of saying hello again.

Three weeks.

The pain remained as fresh as the snow he focused on outside the picture window. A December storm trumpeted a white Christmas, blanketing the ground, bushes, and trees in a pristine mantle. He'd made secret plans for Christmas, plans which included a proposal. He wanted to hang trimmings on a tree with Stacy, and when she placed the star on the top, he wanted to rock the stool she'd be standing on and catch her in his arms. Abruptly, he blocked out the rest of his fantasy.

He'd surprised the realtor by instructing her to break the lease. Not wanting to chance an encounter with Stacy and cause them both embarrassment, he'd returned to his house during the day, when he knew she'd be at school, to gather his clothes and essential papers.

Tucking the dustcloth she'd been using into her pocket, Millie came up behind Kipp to rub the tense knots in his neck. "I think you're running away," she said gently. "Why don't you at least talk with Stacy?"

"No!" He picked up a *National Geographic*, shuffled some pages, then gave up all pretense of interest and put the magazine back on the Lucite table. He was quiet for a time.

"Sorry, sis. I didn't mean to be sharp. There's no point to my speaking with Stacy. She's none of my affair anymore. We agreed on a signal. She's made her decision. What do the French say? *C'est la vie.* That's life."

Millie frowned slightly. As if she sensed that Kipp resented any show of pity, she busied herself fluffing up the pillows on the couch. Then, fishing for the cloth from her apron pocket, she resumed dusting. Her sky-blue eyes were mirror images of Kipp's: thoughtful and concerned, but with one notable difference. Kipp's were streaked with red from the strain of working long hours with little sleep.

"Quitters get what they deserve, or so they say. There's a message there, brother," she said gently.

Kipp laughed, a harsh, guttural sound. He knew what Millie was trying to do in her own convoluted way. They'd always been on the same wavelength.

"There's also a saying somewhere that only a jackass keeps butting his head where he doesn't belong. Stacy doesn't need interference from me. From what I've seen of Harry, he could charm the hairs off a horse."

"That's some kind of charm," Millie agreed.

Kipp rocked back and forth on the balls of his feet. As if to himself, he whispered raggedly, "Yeah, and there's a certain part of a horse's anatomy I wished I'd kicked him in. It would've saved me the trouble of kicking myself for the last three weeks. Anyway, I've decided a nice long vacation's in order. I haven't had one in a year. Now's a good time to take it."

"I hope you aren't planning on leaving before the

hospital's gala banquet, or have you forgotten you're listed on the program as one of the speakers?"

"Oh, damn. I have forgotten," he said, plainly annoyed. "It's this coming weekend too. It completely slipped my mind."

Millie tried to console her moody brother. "Frank and I are looking forward to a night at the country club. The Willows always does a great job. Didn't you tell us a while ago that your partner and his wife are taking part in the fashion show?"

"Yeah, can you imagine? Vito's supposed to be the groom and Bev's the bride, only she's got a nasty cold. I doubt if she'll be able to make it."

Millie bustled around the living room waving the dustcloth at the furniture. She turned and smiled as if she'd just won a match point in chess.

"You know what I think? I think you're going to have a better time that night than you think."

"And I think you've lost your marbles." Kipp cocked a loving eye at his twin. "Since when have I liked dressing up in a monkey suit?"

Millie strolled out of the room calling her answer over her shoulder. "I live in hope, little brother, I live in hope."

Hope was the one thing he'd run out of. "Don't hold your breath, sis."

Stacy shook two aspirin out of the bottle and swallowed them. For the past three weeks she'd put her life on autopilot. She'd gone around in a daze. During the day she went through the motions of teaching by closing her mind to everything other than her students. At night she replayed the dinner fiasco over and over, but she was still thoroughly in the dark.

When she'd raced upstairs to signal Kipp, his room was dark. Thinking he was downstairs, she'd raced across to ring the bell. Surprised to find his house dark, she'd peeked into the garage and saw that it was empty.

Relieved, and certain he'd been called away on an emergency, she'd waited up for him until three in the morning before falling asleep. To her knowledge he'd never returned home.

It was as if he'd fallen off the face of the earth. Repeated calls to his house were rerouted to his office, where she hit a stone wall. A stone wall that included his overprotective secretary, who told her Dr. Palmer was busy with a patient.

Kipp wasn't ill. He hadn't died. He was working. No tragedy had befallen him.

Eventually, humiliated and heartsick, she got the message. She'd told him she loved him. She even talked herself into believing the only reason he hadn't told her he loved her in return was that he was waiting to hear what had happened with Harry.

Twice in her life now she'd made serious mistakes. The ridiculous scene in her house must have scared Kipp off. He'd seen Felicia with another man too.

Without moving, Stacy would lie in bed and wait for her bones to be so weary she'd fall asleep for a few fitful hours. She learned the hard way how little sleep the human body requires to function. But she was coming close to the edge. She'd thinned down to a size six and couldn't afford to lose more weight.

"Fashionably hollow cheeks," Bev said when Stacy had dropped by to see her. "Don't lose any more weight, kiddo." Bev worried about her and she worried about Bev.

"I need a favor." Bev held court amid Kleenex and vaporizer.

"Oh, no, I couldn't!" Stacy cried, hearing Bev's request.

"Please, Stacy? Will you stand in for me? This cold's really decked me."

"I absolutely cannot go to the hospital fund-raiser," Stacy said shrilly. There was hysteria in her voice.

"Stacy," Bev wailed, "I'm letting the whole committee down. The gown was ordered in my size. There's no time for me to start calling around to the other wives, not with such short notice. I don't even know their sizes. Please, as long as we're the same size, you've got to do this for me."

Stacy popped another aspirin into her mouth. She felt like weeping. She was dying by inches at the idea of seeing Kipp again, especially if she was dressed in a bridal gown. She fervently prayed he didn't plan on attending the function. Her one ray of hope was that he'd never mentioned it to her.

"All right," she agreed, wishing it were ten years from now, "but I insist on leaving right after the fashion show."

"You're a peach," Bev said, her eyes watering. "Vito wants to leave early too."

Stacy's next shock came by way of a letter. Ironically her story about the giraffe, the animal she'd patterned after Kipp, was going to be published. It should have been an ecstatic time in Stacy's life. Her first thought was "I've got to tell Kipp." She wanted to share the joy with him, but she discovered that without him to share this pleasure, it meant little to her.

"I've never seen you this way," Pat Lindgren said

sympathetically after the other teachers departed from the teachers' room. Her principal, Mr. Allirtez, told his staff about the sale of Stacy's story. She'd accepted the fuss made over her with as much enthusiasm as a corpse propped up at its own wake.

Although she hadn't any intention of talking about her troubles, she found herself tearfully gulping out the whole story of her divorce and falling in love with Kipp.

"There, there, Stacy. Something tells me there's a piece missing to this puzzle. Kipp loves you. I feel it in my bones."

Stacy sniffed into her handkerchief. Her eyes glittered with tears. "Oh, Pat, you're an old romantic. You've been reading too many books. In real life misery loves company, and I've got plenty of misery."

Pat's steady gaze searched Stacy's upset face. "If Kipp is the man you want in your heart, you have to go after him. Whatever caused him to get cold feet, at least you know it wasn't another woman. Not with the sequence of events coming so rapidly after Harry left. Search your mind. There's a clue there somewhere. You're a writer. Everyone drops clues. People act in character."

Two hours later Stacy was still mulling over Pat's advice, when her doorbell rang. Preoccupied with her thoughts, she opened the door to find Millie standing on the porch with a cup of sugar in her hand and a smile on her lovely face.

"Aren't you going to ask me in? I don't bite."

Dumbfounded, Stacy stepped aside as Kipp's twin breezed into her house. Handing Stacy the cup of sugar, she shrugged out of her lynx coat and dropped it on the nearest chair. Her eyes traveled over her hostess in a slow, thorough perusal.

"That's good," Millie noted approvingly. There were purplish shadows under Stacy's eyes. Her hair was disheveled from plowing her fingers through it, and there was an air of distraction about her.

"That's very good," Millie repeated.

"What is?" Stacy asked frostily. She was put off by the feminine version of Kipp's voice, the similar inflections. Even the compelling cornflower-blue eyes were the same.

"You look as bad as Kipp does," Millie said cheerfully. "That's good. I was afraid I might find you looking well."

Stacy's jaw dropped. Not only was Millie an uninvited guest, she was insulting to boot!

"If you were looking marvelous," Millie continued blandly, "I'd have made up some excuse and gone."

Stacy bristled. She didn't need a comment on her lousy looks. She didn't need anything from Kipp or his family. She'd suffered a carload of humiliation.

"Did Kipp send you? Because if he did—"

"Please," Millie interrupted. "Give me credit for something. The sugar was just an obvious ruse. As I see it, you don't look too happy. Isn't your reconciliation with Harry going well?" she asked carefully.

"What reconciliation?" Stacy felt her heart begin to pound. Her brain registered what Millie said about Kipp looking terrible too.

The two women stared at each other for a moment.

"You're not reconciled," Millie said as if conferring a diploma on Stacy. "Forgive me for smiling like a Cheshire cat, but that's quite wonderful." Her eyes widened impishly. "Oh, my dear, have I got a story for you! Sit down and listen."

Stacy wasn't used to being ordered around, but

curiosity goaded her into silence. Besides, the truth was, there was something refreshing about Millie. Stacy listened with a heightening sense of happiness while Millie explained how miserable Kipp had been and why.

"So you see," Millie concluded, "the man's crazy about you. I'm crazy about him and want him to be happy. I'm also crazy to get that damned dog out of my house which means my beloved brother must go too. You, poor dear, seem eager to have both of them. As a fairy godmother *extraordinaire*, I've come prepared with a possible solution."

Stacy regarded Millie suspiciously, as she waited for all the pieces of the puzzle to be put in place.

"When Kipp mentioned Bev's cold and that he didn't know if she would be able to attend the fundraiser, it gave me an idea. I know you two are friendly."

"So?"

"So, do you know if Bev's still going to be in the fashion show?"

"No. I'm taking her place."

In the role of the perfect conspirator, Millie leaned forward and clasped Stacy's hands. "Super. This couldn't have worked out better. Have you ever heard of the old shell game?"

Who hadn't? "That's when a con man slips a pea under a walnut shell. When the person tries to guess which shell the pea is under, it's always under a different shell."

"Exactly, my dear Watson." Millie flashed a brilliant smile, displaying a dimple identical to her twin's. "Kipp's going to be the replacement pea for Vito, only he doesn't know it yet. Leave that part to me. Now, if you and I pool our talents for chicanery, by the time this is over, you and Kipp will be two peas under the same pod."

Stacy held her hopes in check. "How do you know Kipp's planning on attending?"

"Because," Millie said with the guilelessness of a mother superior, "I took the liberty of reminding him of his professional duty. He's on the program. There's nothing like a nice dose of the guilts to lure a sinner back on track."

Stacy laughed as some of the tension and worry slipped away. Her eyes sparkled. It was a relief to be in cahoots with a worthy cohort. "And in order for this switcheroo plan to work," she offered, recognizing in Millie a true kindred soul, "I'll need to be veiled. It so happens the gown comes with one, and believe me, it's layered. I've seen pictures. It's part of the show. Kipp'll have no idea who the bride is until the last minute."

By the time Millie hugged her good-bye, Stacy almost felt sorry for Kipp. Kipp, the dear, sweet, noble, misguided man whom she loved madly.

Humming "What a Difference a Day Makes," Stacy searched her address book for the phone number of a certain old business acquaintance in Englewood, New Jersey! There was one more piece of business to attend to, something she hadn't even told Millie!

Twelve

Stacy arrived at the Willows Country Club well in advance of the time the members of the Women's Auxiliary and the guest speakers were scheduled to meet to review their parts in the evening's program. She inspected the lavishly decorated banquet room fashioned to resemble an outdoor garden. Chinese orchids and sweetly scented bouquets of hybrid freesia in a riot of colors adorned each table. She also examined the long runway where the models were to parade.

With the help of a dresser from Claudine's Bridal Shop, she was already gowned and waiting. Shortly before she was due to make her appearance, the gown's long train would be attached to the dress by a series of fasteners cleverly hidden in the folds of the silk taffeta material.

Despite all her hopes, she wondered if her plan to see Kipp for the first time in such a public setting would backfire. How could Millie know everything? Maybe Millie read the wrong conclusions into what Kipp said to her. If she had an ounce of brains, she'd return home, lock the door behind her, head for the bottle of aspirin, get in bed, and read a good book.

She was just about to make a dash for the door and beg anyone she saw who approximated her dress size to play Bride for the Night, when the door to the dressing room opened and Kipp's sister poked her head in the room.

"Millie, am I glad to see you. I've been sitting here thinking all sorts of dreadful things. What's Kipp doing now? Do you think he suspects anything?" She fought the impulse to charge out of there anyway.

Millie's expression was placid. She sank down on a chair and kicked off her black evening pumps. "These shoes were made for a pigmy. I swear, my feet grew two sizes since I put them on tonight."

"Millie, please—"

"Stacy, calm down. Trust me. Vito's just asked Kipp to change places with him and there was no way he could refuse at the last minute." Millie opened her gold lamé clutch purse and took out a slim, maroon velvet jewelry box which she handed to Stacy.

"What's this?" Stacy asked, the surprise showing on her face as she released the clasp on the box and saw the contents. The dazzling jewels took her breath away.

"How lovely!" A necklace accented by round and baguette-shaped diamonds lay on the satin interior. "But why?"

Millie kissed her cheek. She squeezed Stacy's ice cold fingers for reassurance.

"For luck. Wear it with the gown. I've got to go now, they're shooing me out of the dressing room. By the way, you look like a dream. Wait till Kipp sees you!" She disappeared in the commotion of doctor's wives gathered in the hallway waiting for the fashion show to begin.

Perplexed by the loan of the expensive necklace, and closeted in the small dressing room, her thoughts crowding in on her, Stacy waited nervously.

Soon, in a deep clear voice, she heard Kipp's plea to the audience for extra donations to help the hospital's fund drive. Hearing his voice for the first time in weeks threw her into a panic. He sounded so dear, so sincere, so warm. She wanted to throttle the noble dope for the hell she'd lived through. Then she wanted to kiss him until he gasped for air.

Francine Dupré, fashion coordinator for Claudine's Bridal Shop, flounced into the room. Reading from a clipboard, Francine reviewed the diagram of the banquet room. In a no-nonsense tone of voice, she discussed her directions with Stacy.

"Brides do not walk, brides glide. Halt at the top of the runway, pivot ever so slowly. The idea is to move so smoothly that the long train on this exquisite, pure silk taffeta gown glides with you. We want the audience to get the full effect of the deep lace border. Is your garter in place? When the groom slides it off your leg we want the audience to see the diamond lace pattern in the shell-pink hosiery."

Stacy assured her persnickety instructress she'd follow the instructions meticulously. She'd glide if it killed her, Stacy promised herself. As to how she'd react when Kipp's magic fingers touched her skin, that was none of Francine's business.

"Good. Naturally, we prefer to use all our own models. However, just this once, for a good cause you know, we pamper the ladies of the auxiliary."

"For a good cause," Stacy repeated, wishing she could pop a soda cracker into her mouth. Her tummy was rumbling, a fact that Francine Dupré acknowledged with a reproving arch of her pencil-thin brows.

"The groom will assist you. He will be awaiting his bride at the side entrance. You will hear the commentator announce his name. It is then and only then that you raise your layered veil for the first time. Mystery—a bride must carry an aura of mystery, *n'est-ce pas?*"

"Mais oui." For more reasons than one, mon Général, Stacy added silently.

"You'll stand with your groom beneath the trellis for the mock wedding ceremony. Do be careful not to let the train get caught in the clematis. We still have to sell the gown, you know."

"Certainement," Stacy said, dredging up her high school French. Her case of nerves vanished as her sense of mischief reasserted itself.

The fashion commentator spoke from the lectern, which was decorated with pink and lavender mini amaryllis. Charlie Lumis's famed society orchestra struck up the accompanying music. The show began.

The commentator introduced the first part of the show. Stacy's appearance was scheduled last, to be the icing on the cake. From behind the scenes she heard the enthusiastic response of the audience.

Knowing this was all in good fun, the members of the large audience responded to each model in high spirits. Away from the serious nature of their profession, the normally sedate doctors fell into the festivities like high school boys at a cheerleaders' competition.

Stacy peeked through the curtain to watch Kipp's reaction to the high jinks. He could have been a monk for all the enthusiasm he showed. She'd seen that pensive look before. He was as tight as a drum.

The people, the music, all the hoopla in the room

faded as she feasted her hungry eyes on him. He was dressed in a black tuxedo with black satin lapels, and the umber tones in his dark brown hair were almost black against the stark white of the ruffled shirt he wore.

His broad shoulders fought a battle with the jacket, filling it to exact proportions. Poor darling, she thought. He looked as if he wished he were somewhere else. It amused her to realize she was glad. She wasn't ready for him to be enjoying himself. Not yet.

Someone came over to whisper something into Kipp's ear and Stacy saw him rise. He headed for the side stairs to the stage. Charlie Lumis tapped his baton and the orchestra struck up the strains of "Here Comes the Bride."

Stacy took a deep breath. She waited as the multilayered veil was adjusted. Head high, she walked through the curtains. Immediately a hush fell over the audience. With their first glimpse of her standing regally at the head of the runway, everyone in the audience seemed suspended in time. It was as if she were truly a bride they'd come to wish well, forgetting this was make-believe.

Then a male voice called out, "Gorgeous," and the spell was broken. A smattering of applause rippled through the banquet room. From beneath her veil Stacy caught a glimpse of Kipp. His brilliant blue eyes seemed amused at the goings-on, and she realized that whatever reason he'd had for not paying attention to the show before vanished in thin air.

He was staring at her with pure male interest, a gleam of humor lighting his blue eyes.

How dare he! He was not supposed to be coming on to another woman!

She felt his eyes follow her as she forced herself to

glide, not walk down the runway while the commentator described the bridal gown in minute detail. At the end of the runway she pivoted slowly, waiting for the helpers to adjust the beautiful lace-edged train.

Chin high, eyes blazing beneath the veil, she walked back up the runway. Kipp moved into position to take her hand. Halting on cue, she turned her head toward him. She stared up into his incredible summer-blue eyes.

The no-good devil was laughing!

"Well, well, what have we here?" Kipp murmured so only the two of them could hear.

His admiring gaze fixed on her heaving breasts, then boldly lowered to her tiny waist.

The commentator signaled to Kipp to raise Stacy's veil.

"And now, ladies and gentlemen," Stacy heard her say, "the part we've all been waiting for. At last, the bride will be unveiled so the groom may cast his eyes on his lady love."

An expectant hush fell over the room.

A trickle of laughter escaped Kipp's mouth. He leaned close to her, his hands already in position at the base of the veil. His knuckles grazed her bare skin. "Shall we show them what they've been waiting for, my lady love?"

His voice was whispery. His warm breath fanned her face as softly as a butterfly's wings. Stacy was plunged into the depths of despair. Kipp, who should have been miserable, was having the time of his rotten life!

"True love, my foot!" she fumed, not caring if the audience stared in fascination as the puffs of air she breathed out forced the veil from the front of her mouth. "You're nothing but a two-timing, low life—"

She never completed her litany of anger. In a flash Kipp removed the veil to a fanfare of music. The audience clapped its appreciation of Stacy's lovely face. And when Kipp swooped down to kiss away the surprise on her lips, applause filled the large room.

He pulled back. "Such awful words on our wedding day, Stacy," he chided her. He curled a silky blond strand of her hair on his finger. "You'll have to clean up your foul language if we're going to be married. I can't have the mother of my children screeching like a fishwife. It's bad enough she can't cook."

Kipp tucked her arm firmly in his to escort her down the runway. She yanked her hand out of his arm. She dug her fists into the waistline of the wedding gown. He had tricked her!

"You knew! You knew it was me all the time, didn't you? Even under those seven veils!" For good measure she jabbed his chest with a red-tipped nail.

"Tut, tut." He picked up the finger jabbing his shirt and kissed it to the uproarious delight of his fellow doctors and their spouses. "You're disappointing our guests." Smiling broadly at the audience, he tucked her hand in his arm again and began to move down the runway.

"I don't give a damn whom I'm disappointing." Calling a halt to the procession, she stamped her ivory satin shoe.

"How did you know?"

Above her the fiery blaze in his eyes was hooded in lazy passion. "Because, my sweet, above those nipples which are right now driving me crazy and providing me with a reason to lift you up and carry you out of here, you're wearing my gift to you."

"Your gift?"

Stacy's hands flew to the diamond nestling at her bosom like a contented babe. Millie!

Stacy zeroed in on the table where Millie and Frank sat beaming at them. Millie tilted her head and threw her hands out in a gesture of acknowledgment.

"That's right, darling." Kipp's arm snaked around Stacy in an embrace. "Blood's thicker than water. After all, she's my twin. I know how she thinks. Ever since we've been kids we've played tricks on other people. I knew she was up to something. It wasn't hard to wangle your little scheme out of her. You two should make quite a pair. Millie, bless my interfering twin, explained everything. I've been a blind fool. Forgive me, my love." His smile was tender as he gazed down at her.

When he put it that way, how could she stay angry? She'd won after all.

"Did I hear you mention marriage?" Stacy asked, a smile teasing the corners of her mouth.

"Don't interrupt my trend of thought. Did I tell you I love you? I do, you know. I don't care if the whole wide world hears it. I love you. You and your zany bundle of tricks have been driving me crazy ever since we met. After we're married we're going to live in a big house surrounded by a moat, with sixteen-foot-high concrete walls topped by an electrically charged barbed-wire fence, and have Connie in command of the guard dogs patrolling along with the uniformed troops."

"Anything else?" Stacy inquired, wondering how such a wacky proposal could sound so marvelous.

"Yes." He kissed the side of her neck while the audience clamored for more. "I forgot the tower. We must have a tower with powerful klieg lights sweeping the property. I'm not taking any more chances with you ever again, love."

"And will my wedding dress have stripes with a large *P* scrawled on the back?"

"Absolutely not. You're going to be naked. I'll paint the stripes on with chocolate syrup and then I'll . . ." He scattered a shower of kisses on her eyes, her cheeks, and her lips before giving her a chance to respond.

"It sounds divine," she said dreamily. Her mouth parted instinctively and she licked her lips.

"Don't do that or we'll consummate this marriage right now in front of all these guests."

Around them pandemonium broke out. Francine Dupré smiled benevolently. The commentator gave up and was oohing and ahhing into the microphone. All eyes were on the fairy tale unfolding on the runway.

"I'll give you my answer at home," Stacy said breathlessly. Poor man. He had so much to learn. Once a trickster, always a trickster.

"In that case, we're leaving." He fished in his pocket for his wallet and drew out a pile of bills.

"What are you doing?"

"Paying for the wedding dress. You don't think I'm going to wait while you take it off. I've waited for you all my life. I'm not waiting a second longer."

"Yes, dear." She might as well start practicing now.

Francine Dupré accepted the payment for the dress and gushed something congratulatory in French.

Millie and Frank's thumbs-up signal wished them both well. Everybody stood up and clapped and whistled.

Charlie Lumis's band struck up a drum roll. In a magical blur the long train on the wedding gown was unhooked by willing hands. Kipp carried Stacy to his waiting car, racing the speed limit until the Jaguar pulled into her driveway.

The lights were blazing in Stacy's bedroom. "Is that who I think it is?" he shouted as he jumped out of the car.

"No, dear." She might as well learn to say that too. She handed Kipp the key to her house. He hadn't paid any attention to her honest disclaimer.

Gathering her up in his arms, Kipp announced defiantly, "I'm going to throw that damn thing out the window."

"Yes, dear," she murmured, nipping at the side of his neck as he carried her up to her room.

She slid out of his arms and watched Kipp yank the cardboard figure around. Smiling smugly, she saw his surprise erupt into booming laughter as he recognized the face on the cardboard dummy.

"Now who's jumping to conclusions, Dr. Jump-to-Conclusions Palmer? I think you turned out rather well, don't you? Of course, you're only eight years old on the picture, but all little boys have to grow up sometime, don't they, darling?"

"Still," Kipp said, wiggling his eyebrows, "he's a bit young for what I have in mind, my little trickster." He turned his cardboard likeness back to the window and pulled down the shades.

His eyes gleamed, challenging hers. She was ready for him with her heart, her body, her whole being.

"Come here," he said softly.

She moved toward him, unconsciously seductive. She eagerly parted the buttons on his shirt. Her fingers splayed over his warm skin. Looking up at him, she knew the fierce devotion in his gaze matched the love in her heart. He would always be her love, her partner, her protector.

When she spoke her voice was an erotic whisper.

"There's the little matter of an article of clothing separating us."

Inch by slow inch she lifted the hem of the wedding dress. She saw his eyes darken with passion as she raised the hem higher and higher to expose a gossamer-clad thigh.

"My champion knight," she whispered. "You're supposed to remove my blue garter."

A possessive heat blazed in his eyes. With deft fingers he slid the garter from her thigh.

"Are you going to marry me and make an honest man of me?"

"Yes, dear."

It really was so easy to say.

THE EDITOR'S CORNER

It's not easy handling six spirited heroines and six "to die for" handsome, sexy heroes each month, but it's fun trying. It's a tough job, but someone has to do it! The truth is there's nothing tough about editing these LOVESWEPTs—our authors are a joy to work with. What's tough is knowing which book to read first! Luckily, we've solved that problem for you by numbering the books. So once again we have six books that explore romance in all its forms—steamy, sensuous, sweet, funny, and heartwarming.

Our first LOVESWEPT for the month, #240 **CAJUN NIGHTS** by Susan Richardson is definitely steamy! It's set in the bayous of Louisiana where our heroine, renowned travel writer Jeannie Kilmartin, is looking for the perfect hideaway for her next story. Instead, she finds dark, brooding Elliot Escudier poling through the water on his handmade boat. Jeannie has to look twice as Elliot appears in the marshes—is he some long lost pirate who's come to claim her? Elliot owns the land that Jeannie is writing about and he's come to claim the land and keep her from printing her article. And he'll do anything to stop her. Jeannie doesn't mind his interference because she adores his dark, sexy looks. Eventually, all thoughts of an article are thrown out the window when the lovers finally succumb to their overwhelming desire.

In **TRAVELIN' MAN** by Charlotte Hughes, LOVESWEPT #241, Dannie Drysdale is whimsical and luscious looking and utterly determined not to fall in love with a traveling man because at last she's put down roots. Brian Anthony is one extraordinary fellow—as handsome as he is sensitive! But alas, he's a salesman on the move who's determined to rise to the top of the corporate ladder. Nothing can stand in his way or keep him in one place for long. Except Dannie! Once Dannie's eccentric father throws the lovers together, Brian's goals change. Then Dannie's resistance is finally broken down by a bad case of chickenpox and by the great guy who's nursing her back to health. The travelin' man and the

(continued)

"stay-put" woman realize that they both want the same thing—each other!

Something funny happened at LOVESWEPT this month—we discovered we had two heroes with the same name. You probably think that the hero's name is John or Joe or Tom, Dick or Harry—a common name that could easily be duplicated. But then you know that our heroes are never common so they never have common names. Can you believe that we have two strong, sexy, devastating Lincolns this month? Well, we do and we'll let you decide which one is more lovable, but we know that's going to be a very tough decision.

In **INTIMATE DETAILS,** by Barbara Boswell, LOVESWEPT #242, Lincoln Scott is the man Vanessa Ramsey's father decides she should marry. Lincoln finds the dazzling temptress a delectable challenge, especially since she won't consider even liking Linc—and her father's interference has turned her into a tigress! But Vanessa finds it harder and harder to ignore Lincoln's dreamboat looks and his fierce caresses. When he touches her heart, Vanessa listens to her feelings and for the first time in her life, she lets herself be loved. There are some of Barbara's wittiest scenes in this delightful love story—such as one in which her father tries to justify his actions and digs himself into a hole a mile deep. Unforgettable.

Joan Elliott Pickart's offering for the month is **KISS ME AGAIN, SAM,** LOVESWEPT #243, a wonderfully humorous and heartwarming romance in which the heroine appears for the first time hanging from the rafters! Read on and find out how she got there and you'll discover that Austin Tyler is a very pretty auburn-haired construction worker hired to repair Sam Carter's house. Sam finds Austin irresistible in both body and mind and he tells her so. But Austin is afraid that once she tells Sam her terrible secret, he won't want her anymore. Could he make her believe that everything about her was precious to him and he loved all the woman she was?

SAPPHIRE LIGHTNING by Fayrene Preston, LOVESWEPT #244 features our second hero named Linc and I must admit I'm torn between the two men! Linc Sinclair

(continued)

is a handsome, healthy jogger with a fantastic body, as well as being a successful businessman with a fabulous art collection. Toni Sinclair was married to his cousin who died accidentally and now that Toni is on her own with her six-month-old son, she's decided never to remarry. She wasn't a great wife the first time around, and she doesn't want to risk failing again. Linc throws a party in her honor welcoming Toni to the family's hometown and while at his house, Toni realizes just how much they have in common. It all begins with a love for art—and ends with Linc's love for one particular beautiful, female artist. Fayrene Preston has once again set a sensuous, romantic scene where two lovers destined for one another will be sure to find their hearts' desires.

Deborah Smith is a new LOVESWEPT author and we're very excited about **JED'S SWEET REVENGE**, LOVESWEPT #245, the story of a sun-bronzed cowboy and the beautiful woman he calls "Wildflower"! Jed Powers leaves Wyoming and heads south for Sancia Island to finally seek his revenge on his dead grandfather. Instead he finds Thena Saint-Colbet—very much alive and a gorgeous free spirit with wild, thick auburn hair. Thena lives on the island that Jed intends to destroy, and she teaches him its beauty. All thought of revenge fades when love takes its place and, in the end, Jed's revenge is sweet.

I'm sure you're going to enjoy Deborah Smith's book and welcome her to the LOVESWEPT family. You have a wonderful month of reading ahead of you, so stay warm and cozy with your favorite LOVESWEPT.

Sincerely,

Kate Hartson

Kate Hartson
  Editor
LOVESWEPT
Bantam Books, Inc.
666 Fifth Avenue
New York, NY 10103

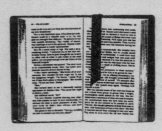